Elizabeth knocked softly. No response. She knocked again and whispered, "Mr. Hounslow?"

"What are you doing?" a voice echoed down the hall.

She jumped and turned. George Betterman had been watching her from the end of the corridor. He put his wheelchair into gear and drove toward her. She wanted to run. "Sheriff Hounslow couldn't find his father at the Village, so I thought I'd check to see if he was here."

"Well, he's not, Sarah, so don't worry your pretty little head about him."

Elizabeth faced Betterman fully. "Why did you call me Sarah?"

A flicker of a smile formed at the corners of his mouth. "It's your name, isn't it?"

"No," she said. "My name's Elizabeth."

"I'm sure that's what they keep telling you. But we know better, don't we?"

Every instinct in Elizabeth's body told her to get away, and get away now. "I think you have me confused with someone else."

The tiny smile stayed frozen beneath his whiskers. "I'm sure that I don't."

Memory's Gate

Paul McCusker

LION
PUBLISHING

Lion Publishing
A Division of Cook Communications
4050 Lee Vance View
Colorado Springs, CO 80918, USA

MEMORY'S GATE
© 1996 by Paul McCusker

First edition 1996

Cover design by Bill Paetzold
Cover illustration by Matthew Archambault

ISBN 0-7459-3613-X

Printed in the United States of America
00 99 98 97 96   5 4 3 2 1

Published in association with the literary agency of Alive Communications, Inc., 1465 Kelly Johnson Blvd., Suite 320, Colorado Springs, CO 80920

Library of Congress Cataloging-in-Publication Data

McCusker, Paul
     Memory's Gate / by Paul McCusker.
          p.   cm. — (Time twists)
     "A Lion book."
     Summary: Fifteen-year-old Elizabeth volunteers in a retirement home where a con man promises the elderly that they can slip through a time fault line and return to their past.
          ISBN 0-7459-3613-X
          [1. Old age—Fiction. 2. Time travel—Fiction. 3. Christian life—Fiction.]   I. Title. II. Series: McCusker, Paul, 1958- Time twists.
PZ7. M47841635Me   1996
[Fic]—dc20
                                96-17155
                                    CIP
                                    AC

To Rob and Di Parsons
for introducing me to St. Fagans
and starting this adventure

What in the world am I doing here? Elizabeth Forde asked herself as she followed a silver-haired woman down the main hallway of the Fawlt Line Retirement Center.

Of all the things I could have spent the rest of my summer doing, why this? Yes, she had agreed to volunteer at the retirement center. She had even felt enthusiastic about the idea at the time. But walking down the cold, clinical, pale green hallway with the smell of pine disinfectant in the air, Elizabeth wondered if she had made a mistake.

She'd been swept along by Reverend Armstrong's passionate call to the young people of the church. He had exuberantly insisted that they get involved in the community. They must be a generation of givers rather than takers, he said. His words had been powerful and persuasive, and before she knew what she was doing she had joined a line of other young people to sign up for volunteer service. Just a few hours a day, three or four days a week, for a couple of weeks. It hadn't sounded like much.

An old man, bent like a question-mark, stepped out of his room and smiled toothlessly at her.

It's too much, she thought. *Let me out of here.*

"I know what you're thinking," said her guide, Mrs. Kottler, with a smile. "You're thinking that a few hours a day simply won't be enough. You'll want more time. Everyone feels that way. But if you do the best you can with the hours you have, you'll be just fine. I promise. Maybe later, we'll let you come in longer."

Elizabeth smiled noncommittally.

Mrs. Kottler wore masterfully applied makeup, discreet gold jewelry, and a fashionable dark blue dress. She smelled of expensive perfume. Elizabeth thought she looked more like a real estate agent than the administrator of an old folks home.

"We don't call it an 'old folks home,' by the way," Mrs. Kottler said, as if she'd read Elizabeth's mind, "or a 'sanitarium' or any of those other outdated names. It's just what the sign says: it's a retirement center. People have productive and active lives here. Being a senior citizen doesn't mean you have one foot in the grave. People who retire at sixty-five often have another twenty or thirty years to enjoy their lives. We're here to help them do it as well as it can be done."

Elizabeth noted a couple of productive and active people staring blankly at the television sets in their rooms.

"Of course, we do have *older* residents who have gone beyond their mental or physical capacity to jog around the center six times a day, if you know what I mean," Mrs. Kottler added as they rounded a corner and walked briskly down a short corridor toward two large doors. "For the rest of them, there's a full schedule of activities throughout the day. Most take place here in the recreation room."

Without missing a beat, she pushed the two doors. They swung open grandly to reveal a large room filled with game tables, easels, bookcases filled with hundreds of books and magazines, and a large-screen television. Unlike the main halls and cafeteria Elizabeth had just seen, this room was decorated warmly with wooden end tables, lace doilies, and the kinds of chairs and sofas found in showcase living rooms. Tastefully painted scenes of sunlit hills, lush green valleys, and golden rivers adorned the walls.

"Pretty, huh? I decorated this one myself," Mrs. Kottler said. "I know what you're thinking. You're thinking that they should have let me decorate the entire center. Well, that wasn't my decision to make. The residents are responsible for decorating their own rooms any way they like. Most of the other assembly areas were done before I joined the staff."

"How long have you been working here?" Elizabeth asked politely.

"Five years," Mrs. Kottler answered, then added wistfully, "It goes by so quickly, don't you find?"

For Elizabeth, who had been only ten years old when Mrs. Kottler started her job, the last five years hadn't gone by quickly at all. She had traveled from the carefree days of Barbie dolls to the insecurities of middle school to the early stages of womanhood and wide-eyed wonder over her future. Oh—and she had also traveled to a parallel time. That was all. If she could have answered Mrs. Kottler honestly, she'd have said, *No, it hasn't gone by very quickly*. And as she considered the residents of the center and realized that one day *she* might have to live in a place like this, she hoped life would never go by quickly. She shivered.

A tall, handsome young man entered through a door at the opposite end of the recreation room. "Mrs. K., I was wondering—"

"Doug Hall, come meet Elizabeth Forde," Mrs. Kottler said, waving her arms as if she might create enough of a breeze to drag Doug over to them.

Doug strode across the room with a smile that showed off the deep dimples in his cheeks. *He's a movie star*, Elizabeth thought. His curly brown hair, perfectly formed face, large brown eyes, and a build that was enhanced, not hidden, by the white clinical coat made her certain. *He's a movie star playing a doctor*, she amended.

Doug reached her with an outstretched hand and said, "Well, my enjoyment of this place just increased by a hundred percent."

She shook his hand and blushed. "Hi."

"Doug is our maintenance engineer," Mrs. Kottler explained.

Doug smiled again. "She means I'm the main janitor. But I'm more like a bouncer, in case these old madcap merrymakers get out of control with their wild partying and carousing."

"Stop it, Doug," Mrs. Kottler giggled. Then she turned to Elizabeth. "I know what you're thinking. You're thinking, what's a good-looking and charming young man like him doing in a place like this?"

For once, Mrs. Kottler had it right. *He's a movie star playing a janitor?* It didn't seem appropriate somehow. She waited for the answer.

"Well, if you can find out, please let me know," Mrs. Kottler said with another giggle. "He won't tell anyone. I assume he has a deep, dark secret. Perhaps he was involved in some sort of intrigue in France and barely escaped from the police on his yacht. Why else would he be hiding in a retirement center in a small town?"

"If you have to know the truth, I ran off with the church funds," Doug said. He and Mrs. Kottler chuckled as if this little exchange had been their own private joke for a long time.

Doug rested his gaze on Elizabeth. Suddenly she wondered how she appeared to him. How did she look in her freshly issued white-and-pink clinic jacket—frumpy or professional? Had she taken pains with her makeup? Were her large brown eyes properly accented? Did her smile look natural? Her skin was freshly tanned, no unsightly pimples, which made her glad. She had tied back her long brown hair, but now she wished she had let it fall loose. It looked better that way, Jeff always said.

Jeff.

The thought of her boyfriend derailed her train of thought. For a fraction of a second she felt as though she had been unfaithful. She glanced away from Doug self-consciously.

"Back to business," Doug said pleasantly, as if he'd picked up on her feelings and wanted to spare her any embarrassment. "I was wondering if now would be a good time to adjust the settings on the Jacuzzi. You don't have any plans to let the kids in this afternoon, right?"

"No, Doug, the 'kids' won't be going in today," Mrs. Kottler replied. "Do whatever you need to do."

He nodded. "Maybe Elizabeth will want to test it later when I'm finished." He gave her a coy grin.

"I think Elizabeth will be too busy getting acclimated to her new duties," Mrs. Kottler replied.

Doug tipped a finger against his brow as a farewell. "If there's anything I can do to help . . ."

Mrs. Kottler watched him go. "He's such a flirt. A charming, good-looking flirt, but a flirt nonetheless." Elizabeth detected a hint of a sigh in her voice.

The tour of the center eventually led Elizabeth and Mrs.

Kottler outside to the two acres of manicured grounds, landscaped into gentle green slopes that ultimately rolled down to a small manmade lake called Richards Pond. It was surrounded by a natural forest that extended off to the horizon. The humidity of the August afternoon was oppressive. Elizabeth felt as though she'd just stepped into a sauna.

"The heat tends to keep everyone inside with the air conditioning," Mrs. Kottler said.

"Except those two," Elizabeth said, gesturing to two people in a white Victorian-style gazebo near the lake.

"That's Sheriff Hounslow and his father," Mrs. Kottler said with just enough annoyance to betray her usual professional detachment. "I suppose we should say a quick hello."

As they got closer, Elizabeth saw that the sheriff, a large man in a light gray uniform, was pacing in an agitated way. His father, a shadow from this distance, was sitting on one of the benches that lined the gazebo. Sheriff Hounslow saw them coming and waved.

Mrs. Kottler spoke to Elizabeth in a low voice, "Adam Hounslow joined us just a couple of days ago. Like many new residents, he's having a hard time adjusting. Hello, Sheriff!"

Mrs. Kottler and Elizabeth mounted the steps to the shade of the round white roof covering the gazebo. The heat and humidity were no less noticeable there.

"Look who's here," Sheriff Hounslow announced. "Mrs. Kottler and—well, well—Elizabeth Forde."

"Oh, you know my new volunteer. Elizabeth will be with us a few hours a day for the next couple of weeks."

"How nice. You be sure to take special care of my father," the sheriff said. "His name is Adam."

Elizabeth could see the old man clearly now. He was bent like a weeping willow with wisps of thin white hair sprayed out from a wrinkled face. Only in the eyes—hazel and currently encased in deep frowns—could she see a resemblance between the father and the son.

"Wouldn't you like a pretty girl like Elizabeth to help take care of you, Dad?" the sheriff asked.

"I don't need to be taken care of," the old man growled. He tucked his head down against his chest.

Sheriff Hounslow ignored the remark and continued, "I'm surprised to see you here, Elizabeth. Shouldn't you be getting ready for the grand opening of that Historical Village, or whatever Malcolm calls it?"

The Historical Village, created by Malcolm Dubbs out of his own vast financial resources, was dedicated to capturing periods of history through authentic buildings, displays, and artifacts that he'd brought in from all over the world. From picture frames and hairbrushes to school houses and church ruins, as much as he could collect from the past few hundred years was represented.

Elizabeth was annoyed at this rather tactless reminder of something she'd given up to help out at the retirement center. It didn't help her mood.

"I didn't know you were connected to Malcolm Dubbs!" Mrs. Kottler said, apparently impressed.

"She goes out with Malcolm's nephew, Jeff," the sheriff informed her.

"Do you? Doug will be very disappointed," Mrs. Kottler teased. "When does the Village formally open?"

"Phase One opens on Saturday," Elizabeth answered.

"Phase One?"

"Uncle Malcolm—" Elizabeth stopped herself, realizing how strange it must sound for her to use the name she'd always known him by. "Malcolm says the Village is a work in progress. He'll open various sections of it as they're ready."

"It's a Disneyland of history," the sheriff said flippantly. Sheriff Hounslow had had a few run-ins with Malcolm, two of them related to unexplainable and bizarre time-travel episodes. Hounslow flat-out refused to believe they had happened. Elizabeth also suspected that the sheriff was jealous of Malcolm's wealth and the respect he commanded from the townspeople. But whatever the reason, Hounslow never missed an opportunity to poke fun at

Malcolm's projects or eccentricities. "I can't wait to go on the rides!"

"Are there rides?" Mrs. Kottler asked, amazed.

Elizabeth shook her head. "No. Just buildings and displays."

Sheriff Hounslow grinned. "There's going to be a big celebration. The mayor will be there and a special assistant to the governor, and there'll be a telegram from the president and maybe even world peace—all thanks to Malcolm Dubbs."

"Don't be such a pompous fool, Richard," Adam Hounslow barked at his son. "I'm looking forward to seeing the Village."

"I'm glad you're looking forward to something," the sheriff remarked.

"Living in a place like this, I'm lucky to look forward to anything," Adam snapped.

"You don't mean that," Mrs. Kottler interceded. "The Fawlt Line Retirement Center will be like home to you in no time at all, I promise."

Adam scowled at her. "This will never be my home. My home has been sold right out from under me by my thoughtful and compassionate son."

"I'm not getting into this argument with you again, Dad," Hounslow said irritably.

"Yes you will," Adam replied. "As long as you force me to live in places where I don't want to live, we'll have this argument."

The sheriff turned on his father. "Where else are you going to live? You couldn't stay in that big old place alone. You can barely take care of yourself, let alone a big house. Do I have to remind you of what led up to this? Do I have to announce to the whole world how you nearly burnt the house down—twice—by forgetting to turn the stove burners off? Or the time you flooded the house by wandering off to the store while the bath water was running?"

Mrs. Kottler jerked her head at Elizabeth, signaling that they should leave. Heading across the grounds, Elizabeth could still hear the voices of the two men arguing.

"I know what you're thinking," Mrs. Kottler said. "You're thinking that Adam must be crazy not to like our center. Well, I agree. But he'll get used to it. They always do."

They approached the building from the back, where a stone patio had been added to the recreation room. It was congested with plants and flowers of all kinds. A man in a wheelchair was pruning the plants, meticulously spraying the leaves and wiping them with a water bottle. He had long, gray hair that poured out from under a large baseball cap. Beneath the brim of the cap he wore sunglasses so dark that she couldn't see his eyes at all. A bushy mustache and beard followed downward. It struck Elizabeth that, apart from his cheeks, his face couldn't be seen at all. He wore a baggy jogging suit that made her think he must be roasting inside.

Mrs. Kottler introduced him as Mr. Betterman, another new resident. He grunted and held a carnation out to her.

"He wants you to take it," Mrs. Kottler whispered.

Elizabeth crossed the patio to the curious-looking man and reached out to take the flower. For a second he didn't let go, but merely said with a half-smile, "I know who you are" and turned away to fiddle with the planter.

Disconcerted, Elizabeth joined Mrs. Kottler again, and they walked inside. She didn't say so, but something about the half-smile and the voice seemed familiar to her.

"That's quite an honor," Mrs. Kottler said, once they were clear of Betterman's hearing. "He doesn't usually talk to anyone. He's a little eccentric."

As they drifted through the recreation room, Elizabeth wondered if she would see Doug again. Then she rebuked herself for caring. She wasn't normally a flirtatious person—nor was she interested in anyone but Jeff—and yet . . .

Mrs. Kottler smiled contentedly. "Well, that's most of it. I know what you're thinking. You're thinking that this is more like a beautiful hotel than a retirement center. We do our best. Now, let me show you where the storage closets are and introduce you to your new responsibilities."

CHAPTER 2

Malcolm Dubbs lived in a cottage on the edge of the Dubbs
family's enormous estate, bordering the north edge of Fawlt Line.
Malcolm was the last in a long line of Dubbs adults, while Jeff, his
nephew, was the last of the line, period. Jeff's parents—Malcolm's
brother and his wife—had died in a plane crash a couple of years
before. That's why Jeff lived in the cottage with his Uncle Malcolm,
and why he took Elizabeth there that evening after he picked her
up at the retirement center.

Uncle Malcolm, tall and slender, was sitting at the large desk
in his den when Jeff and Elizabeth arrived. The sun was soon to
set, and a dim yellow light washed the cluttered room. Thanks to
the oak tree just beyond the French doors leading out to the patio,
drops of cooler, green light filtered into the room. They highlighted
the old-fashioned furniture and skimmed along the dark wood
paneling, the classic paintings, the shelves sagging under too many
books. Jeff smiled and turned on the banker's lamp at the head of
the desk.

Uncle Malcolm looked up and blinked. "Oh, hi," he said
wearily. Preparations for the grand opening of the Historical
Village had left him with too much to do and too little time. At that
moment, he was looking over a daily report of completed projects
within the Village, and another report discussing the security system and inherent weaknesses that might leave some areas vulnerable to theft.

"How's it going?" Jeff asked.

"The security cameras still aren't working." Malcolm leaned
back in his chair, stretching his long body as far as it would go.
"But the eighteenth-century windmill from Holland *is*. And we
wrapped up the construction on the miners' row houses from
southwest Pennsylvania. I'm particularly proud of that exhibit."

"Why that one?" Elizabeth asked.

Malcolm smiled. "Because it shows the chronology of change

15

better than most of the displays. You start at one end of the row houses, and as you walk through each one you'll see exactly how the miners lived during the last 180 years. Go in the first door, and you'll see how it was in 1820. Move on to the next door and you're looking at 1840, then 1860 and 1880 and so on until you come to the present day. We spent a long time getting every detail just right."

Elizabeth shook her head. "I don't know how you pulled it all together."

"Sometimes I wonder myself," Malcolm admitted. "It's been a long time in the making."

"Hundreds of years, I figure," Jeff said.

Malcolm waved his hand as if brushing away the subject. "Forget about the Village for now. How was your first day as a volunteer, Elizabeth?"

Elizabeth was pleased that he even remembered, with all the other demands on his mind. She shrugged. "It was mostly just a time to look around. I only met a couple of people. The center is nice, I guess, if you have to live in a place like that."

Malcolm chuckled. "Your faint praise is overwhelming."

Jeff dropped himself onto the sofa next to Elizabeth and ran his hands through his wavy dark hair. "She's sorry she ever volunteered."

Elizabeth rebuked him with a sharp look.

"What?" Jeff asked innocently. "Did I say something wrong?"

Malcolm stood up and smiled sympathetically. "If it's any consolation, Elizabeth, I think volunteering to help out at a retirement center is a noble and difficult thing to do. Many retirement homes are downright depressing, and elderly people can be very unpredictable, depending on their states of minds. But if you remember that they're people, and not just old people, you'll do them a world of good."

Elizabeth thought of how Doug Hall called them "kids" and probably charmed the socks off them, if only because he didn't treat them differently from anyone else.

"As quirky as your parents are, you should feel right at home." Jeff laughed, and Elizabeth jabbed him with her elbow in reply.

Malcolm tugged at his ear thoughtfully. "I haven't been out to the center since they renovated it. When I was a kid, it wasn't a retirement home; it was just a house on a farm owned by someone the two of you know."

Elizabeth and Jeff looked at each other blankly.

"That's where the Richards property is," Malcolm said. "It's where Charles Richards disappeared."

Elizabeth's and Jeff's mouths fell open.

"You mean *the* Charles Richards?" Jeff asked.

"*My* Charles Richards?" Elizabeth added in disbelief.

Malcolm nodded. The three of them looked at each other silently as the story and the memories came back.

For years the remarkable case of Charles Richards was whispered about around Fawlt Line, but treated as an unsolved mystery by those who investigate such things. Most people considered it one of those small-town myths that make their way into the consciousness of the locals—particularly parents who want to scare their kids into behaving. But Malcolm, Elizabeth, and Jeff believed every word of it, and for very good reasons.

The story went that in the mid-1950s, Charles Richards, the son of a wealthy merchant, settled with his wife and two children on a modest farm outside of Fawlt Line. One morning, the two children were playing next to the sidewalk leading from the house to the front gate. Charles and his wife, Julia, stepped out of the front door, where Charles kissed his wife good-bye. He was leaving to run a few errands in Fawlt Line. Charles walked down the steps toward his children and patted them on their heads as he passed. As he reached the front gate, a car came up the road toward the house. In it was Dr. Hezekiah Beckett, the local veterinarian, and a young boy who was helping the doctor that summer. Charles waved at the doctor, paused to check the time on his wristwatch, then turned as if he might head along the fence to greet the approaching car. He took three steps and, in full view of his wife, his children, Dr. Beckett, and the boy, he disappeared.

Horrified, the five of them raced to the spot and looked around. They saw only the fence and the grass. There were no bushes or trees for him to hide behind, no holes to fall into, nothing to explain how he could simply vanish into thin air.

Dr. Beckett and Julia Richards searched everywhere. Then the townspeople helped. They even dug up the ground where Charles had disappeared, in the belief that he'd fallen into a sinkhole or underground cavern and was trapped below. The ground was solid. Charles was gone. An investigation over the next few weeks failed to establish any clues or conclusion. There was no explanation for it. Julia was bedridden for months, lost in the hope that her husband would return. No funeral or memorial service was ever held. A year later, the family sold the farm and moved away.

For Malcolm, who was the young boy in the car, it was only the beginning of the story. He spent years studying theories of time travel, parallel universes, and alternative dimensions in the belief that he'd find an explanation. All he wound up with were theories and a deep suspicion that Fawlt Line wasn't on a geographical fault, but a *time* fault.

Elizabeth had provided the missing pieces just a few months ago. While taking a bath one night, she had somehow slipped through one of the so-called time faults into a parallel Fawlt Line, switching places with a "time twin" named Sarah, who looked the same as her but had a different personality and life history. In that other time everyone thought she was either an amnesiac or insane. Then she met Charles Richards, who knew how she felt because he had made the same journey. He helped her and, ultimately, saved her life. Elizabeth eventually made it back, thanks to Jeff and Malcolm. But Charles didn't.

Elizabeth still got upset when she thought of Charles trapped in a world that wasn't his own. She hardly talked about—

or even thought about—her time-travel experience, and this discussion was more than she was prepared to deal with. In the deepest part of her heart, she feared that the nightmare might return just by invoking its name.

"They tore down Charles's house and built a gaudy mansion on the site," Malcolm went on to say. "It was the kind of place kids liked to throw rocks at. Then they tore *that* down and put up the new building a couple of years ago. How does it look?"

Elizabeth didn't answer.

"Bits?" Jeff asked, concerned.

Elizabeth snapped back. "Huh? It's . . . modern. Just one story with a lot of hallways. More like a hospital than a home," Elizabeth observed, then thought of Charles again and said no more.

Jeff and Malcolm glanced warily at each other.

"Maybe you should take her home," Malcolm suggested.

Jeff agreed.

Jeff brought his Volkswagen to a squeaky stop in front of Elizabeth's house and turned off the headlights. They both looked up and saw, through the front window, Alan Forde pacing in the living room. He was waving his hands and talking animatedly.

"Is he lecturing someone?" Jeff asked.

Elizabeth shook her head. "Sort of. He's been recording a series of talks about the legends of King Arthur."

"Recording them for whom?"

"Whoever wants them," she answered. "He's been obsessed with Arthur ever since . . . well, you know."

The "you know" was a reference to another adventure—this one shared by Jeff, Malcolm, and Alan Forde with a man who showed up in Fawlt Line one night claiming to be King Arthur himself.

"I'd like to hear him," Jeff said.

Elizabeth glanced at Jeff gratefully. "He'd be happy if you asked."

"I'll wait. Meanwhile, I want you to tell me what's going on with you."

Elizabeth hadn't expected such a direct question, though she should have. Jeff could always tell when something was wrong. Sometimes it was a comfort to her. At other times it made her feel uneasy, particularly when she didn't have an answer . . . like tonight. "I don't know," she said after a long pause.

"You must have a clue," he probed.

She turned in the seat to face him. "I really don't know, Jeff. Maybe it's just volunteering at the center. It was so . . . strange. At first I thought it was because I don't know anything about helping old people. But . . ."

"But what?"

She struggled over what to say next. "Sheriff Hounslow's father is a resident there, and the two of them were arguing and it was embarrassing . . . and then I met a guy in a wheelchair who gave me a carnation, and he said he knew me."

Jeff grimaced. "He knows you? How?"

"He didn't say, and I was too surprised to ask. It was really weird. I had this feeling that I'd seen him before, but I don't know where."

Jeff took her hand in his and spoke softly. "Look, Uncle Malcolm's probably right. Old folks can be unpredictable, and that makes you nervous. Do you remember how Grandpa Dubbs was before he died?"

Elizabeth nodded. "He kept accusing the servants of stealing things."

"Because he kept forgetting where he put them," Jeff finished. "It used to scare the wits out of me when he launched into one of his tirades. Maybe the guy in the wheelchair really thought he knew you, but he was thinking of someone else. Probably someone from a long time ago."

Elizabeth agreed silently.

"And I'm just guessing, but it gave you the creeps to find out that the retirement center was built on Charles Richards' place, right?"

"It brought back a lot more than I wanted to remember."

"That's what I figured." Jeff was quiet for a moment. His expression told Elizabeth that he was forming his words carefully before speaking. "Maybe . . . you should get some counseling about what happened to you. Maybe we all should. Getting bounced around in time and going through what you went through . . . it can't be healthy. Especially since you don't like to talk about it."

"I'm okay," Elizabeth insisted. "I think it's just today, volunteering at the center, bumping into some weird people, and then thinking about Charles Richards. I'll be all right. Really."

She had a hard time going to sleep that night. Images of Charles Richards spun and mixed with scenes from the Fawlt Line Retirement Center. Mrs. Kottler kept saying, "I know what you're thinking," and then Doug Hall offered her flowers carefully pruned by George Betterman in a wheelchair. The floor opened up to expose a dark cavernous time fault that threatened to pull her in. She fell—and never stopped falling.

Elizabeth suddenly sat up in her bed and knew that one way or another she had to take back her offer to volunteer at the center.

Elizabeth spent most of the next day trying to figure out how to gracefully get out of helping at the retirement center. She knew her parents expected her to be more responsible than to quit without a good reason. The challenge was to find that *good* reason. School hadn't started yet, so she couldn't blame homework. She had no other jobs or commitments, so she couldn't say her schedule was too busy. One by one she raised up excuses. One by one her better judgment knocked them down.

Even up to the point when her mother dropped her off at the center, she was thinking of reasons why she should give Mrs. Kottler immediate notice. Despondently she kissed her mother on the cheek and climbed out of the car. Her only hope was that something might happen during her shift that would provide a solid way out.

Mrs. Kottler gave her a simple assignment to start with: take the cart around and fill the water jugs in the rooms.

Elizabeth guessed that this was a standard job for new volunteers and a shrewd way to help them get to know the residents. Many were up and about when Elizabeth walked into the various rooms and assembly areas. It was her first full view of the people she would be mingling with. While some were kind and welcoming, others regarded her with wariness or skepticism. *Just like kids on the first day of school,* she thought. *You can't tell about people until you get to know them better.* That was a good way to think about them, she decided. They were just older kids watching a new student.

But these "students" sure looked different from the ones at school. Elizabeth was instantly struck by the crowns of white hair and varying styles of hairpieces worn by both the men and women. Her next impression was that many were quite agile, moving quickly and freely up and down the hallway, in and out of chairs, without the stiff or stooped gait she expected from older people. Some used canes and walkers, others simply steadied themselves against whatever sturdy objects happened to be nearby. *They're people*, Elizabeth was reminded as they chatted amiably among themselves or played games in the recreation room or strolled thoughtfully alone. There were others, of course, who were less capable and needed more attention and care. Sharp minds were encased in fragile bodies. Sharp bodies sometimes encased fragile minds. It varied from room to room, person to person.

The most uncomfortable moment came when she reached Adam Hounslow's room. The door was slightly ajar, and she could see through the crack that the room was dark. The blinds had been drawn, and Adam was talking to someone in a wheelchair. Though his back was to her, Elizabeth recognized the telltale baseball cap and knew it was George Betterman. The men spoke in low voices. Elizabeth was unsure whether to knock, clear her throat, or simply walk in. She paused in her indecision.

Adam handed something to George, who quickly shoved it under his loose-fitting jogging jacket. The hushed voices and quick action told Elizabeth that she wasn't supposed to be seeing what she was seeing. She turned to sneak away, but banged the four-wheel cart against the wall. The jugs and glasses rattled, and the two men to spun around to face her.

"Sorry to interrupt," she stammered nervously, "but Mrs. Kottler asked me to bring some fresh water."

Adam looked particularly guilty. "I don't need fresh water," he growled.

"I'm sorry," Elizabeth said again and retreated back into the hallway. With shaking hands, she grabbed the handle on the cart. Why was she so nervous? What was it about the men that scared her so?

She heard a soft whirring sound behind her. Seconds later, George Betterman navigated his electric wheelchair past her, pausing to look up at her through the black circles of his sunglasses. *I know who you are*, she expected him to say again. But he didn't say a word. He rode on down the hallway.

Elizabeth closed her eyes, trying to calm the irrational fear that gripped her. A heavy hand fell on her shoulder, and she nearly jumped out of her skin.

"Whoa, now, calm down," Sheriff Hounslow said. "I didn't mean to scare you."

"I'm a little jumpy," Elizabeth admitted quickly.

"I guess you are. Is everything all right?"

"Yeah," she said. "First-day jitters."

"I thought yesterday was your first day."

"Excuse me," she said and raced away with the cart. Before she rounded the next corner, she heard the sheriff greet his father. Adam Hounslow launched the first assault by complaining about his room.

Safely down the next hallway, she stopped again to take a deep breath. *This is stupid*, she told herself. *There's nothing to be afraid of. It was just two old men talking.* She rebuked herself for being so weird and, after a moment, continued her rounds.

The rooms—or *apartments*, as Mrs. Kottler called them—varied in their looks. A few looked sterile and hospital-like. Others reflected attempts by the residents or their families to liven them up with a few sticks of furniture, knickknacks, mementos, souvenirs, and treasures. If awards were given for the homiest room, Frieda Schultz would have won hands down.

From the moment Elizabeth stepped into Frieda's room, she felt transported out of the retirement center into a cozy bungalow. The room was colorful, with bright floral-patterned curtains, and lampshades, and the smell of a light perfume that made her think of lilacs. A chaise lounge had been placed in the corner, smothered with pillows that Frieda had probably made herself, Elizabeth guessed, and a quilt that looked older than anything or anybody in the center. The windowsill was covered with greeting cards, fashion magazines, catalogues, and books by authors like Baroness Orczy and Georgette Heyer and Elswyth Thane—people Elizabeth had never heard of. Victorian tapestries did their best to hide the institutional-white walls. An oak wardrobe with elaborately carved edging along the top and bottom replaced the plain pressed-wood box the center issued. The matching bureau and vanity table, squeezed in along the opposite wall, were overrun with costume jewelry, evening purses, scarves, gloves, perfume bottles, jars, cold cream, tubes, magnifying mirror, boxes, and silver combs and brushes. It gave Elizabeth the impression that Frieda might suddenly decide to call her chauffeur and go out to the theater for the evening.

"I know, I know, it's a cluttered mess," Frieda said from the bathroom door in the corner.

Elizabeth realized she'd been standing in the middle of the room, staring. "I think it's wonderful," she said.

"Well, aren't you the kind one to say so." Frieda, a heavyset woman in a silk housecoat, sashayed into the room as if she were making an entrance at a formal ball dressed in chiffon and lace. Her beauty had faded, but she exuded a poise and charm that had not. "Tell me your name, child."

"I'm Elizabeth. I'm here to give you some fresh water."

"A new volunteer?"

Elizabeth nodded as she flipped open the top on the copper-colored jug. Empty. She retrieved the large jar from the cart and poured water from one to the other.

"You must be traumatized," Frieda said. "A pretty young girl like you thrown in with all these fossils. What in the world are you doing here?"

"I volunteered through my church."

"And regretted it every minute since, I'll bet," Frieda laughed.

Elizabeth answered with a guilty smile.

Frieda returned the smile. "If it's any consolation, I'm very happy to meet you. I get so tired of old people. And you're a churchgoer, too. All the better. I'd go to church if it weren't such a major production."

Elizabeth was surprised. "Production? What makes it a production?"

"I'm not about to bore you with my health problems. We have a chapel here that I can pray in. That'll do for now." Frieda pushed aside some of the pillows on the chaise lounge. "Put down those water jugs and come sit."

"But Mrs. Kottler wants me to—"

"Forget Mrs. Kottler," Frieda said. "I want you to sit down right here and tell me all about yourself. I don't get to meet real people very often and, when I do, I want to know their stories."

Elizabeth shyly sat down on the lounge.

Frieda sat on the opposite end, leaned back and tucked one leg under her large frame. "Comfy? Now . . . what's your story?"

Elizabeth talked. She couldn't help it. Any lull, any missing pieces, any evasion, and Frieda asked just the right question to set it straight. Elizabeth told about her life in Fawlt Line, her friendship with Jeff that eventually led to their dating, her parents, her friends at school.

At varying points, Frieda would drop in her own memory of a similar experience she'd had when she was Elizabeth's age. Elizabeth didn't mind. She found comfort in knowing that her experiences weren't unique only to her, but that a woman four times her age felt the same.

After a half hour, Elizabeth started to get up. She knew Mrs. Kottler would be looking for her.

"Wait," Frieda said and placed a soft hand on Elizabeth's arm. "There's something you haven't told me." Her gaze was penetrating.

"What do you mean?" Elizabeth asked feebly.

"I have a sense about these things—a *gift*, in a way. You're holding something back."

Elizabeth glanced away nervously. Frieda was right; Elizabeth hadn't mentioned her time-travel nightmare. Having made a friend in the center, she wasn't eager to lose her by talking like a lunatic. "Yeah, but it's crazy. I can't talk about it now."

Frieda watched her for a moment, then decided to let the subject drop. "All right. We have time. Other days, other talks, and maybe you'll want to tell me about it. I feel that somehow you *should* tell me. Maybe there are secrets I can tell you, too."

Elizabeth was tempted to take her invitation and pour out the whole tale on the spot, but just then Mrs. Kottler appeared in the doorway.

"There you are!" she exclaimed. "I need your help in the recreation room. There aren't enough judges for the Twister contest!"

Frieda insisted that Elizabeth could go only if she escorted her into the recreation room. "My ankles are hurting today," she complained and sat down in a wheelchair that was waiting behind the door.

Elizabeth happily grabbed the wheelchair handles and whisked Frieda away, the smell of sweet perfume trailing back to her.

"Your ankles?" she asked as she pushed Frieda down the hall.

"I have occasional bouts with arthritis. Not today, actually, but I didn't want to let you go just yet," Frieda replied.

The recreation room was filled with residents, many of whom Elizabeth had seen on her rounds. They sat at the card tables, on the sofas and chairs, engaged in different games and hobbies. At the opposite end of the room, Elizabeth saw Doug Hall in earnest conversation with George Betterman.

"Oh," she said, without meaning to.

Frieda turned around to look at Elizabeth's expression, then followed her gaze over to the two men. "I see," she said with a smile. "Handsome, isn't he? But watch out for him."

"I'm with Jeff," she reminded her newfound friend.

"Of course you are. But your protest tells me you've noticed Doug," Frieda said. "I'm sure he's already flirted with you. No pretty girl goes through here without his pouring on the charm."

"I talked to him for a minute yesterday."

Frieda smiled. "Uh-huh. It's nice, isn't it—having a handsome young man pay attention to you? Even if you both know nothing will come of it."

"I guess."

"Just be certain that nothing *does* come of it, my dear," Frieda warned.

"What do you mean?"

"I get feelings about him. He's a charmer, and the charmers are the ones who can hurt you the worst."

Doug and George Betterman parted, and George headed out to the patio.

Elizabeth knelt closer to Frieda. The lilac perfume lightly tickled her nose. "Do you know Mr. Betterman?" she asked.

Frieda folded her arms across her chest as if she were trying to contain a shiver. "As much as I care to," she said.

"You don't like him?"

"I don't know him well enough to like or dislike him. I know only my impressions."

"What're your impressions?"

She thought for a moment. "How can I put it in terms you'll understand? He gives me the creeps. There's something about him that seems . . ." Her voice trailed off.

Elizabeth waited. When Frieda didn't continue, Elizabeth pressed her. "Seems what?"

"Evil."

CHAPTER 4

Elizabeth is in the bath, chin-deep in warm, relaxing water. She lifts up her right foot just as a drop of water falls from the tap. It splashes cold against her skin. She sighs and closes her eyes.

Why was she in the bath? she suddenly wondered. She had gone to bed.

Instantly, rough hands grab her, hard fingers wrap around her throat, pressing tight, pushing her under icy water.

Alarmed, Elizabeth gasped and struggled to open her eyes. She shouldn't be in the bathtub, but she was. Just like the night she'd slipped through the time fault. It was happening again!

She glances down into the bath and recoils, jerking her legs up.

The water is filthy brown with bits of grass and sludge floating on top, as if a sewer has backed up through the drain. Her stomach turns, and she grabs the sides of the tub to pull herself out. She pushes but can't get her footing on the slick porcelain. Her legs splay out and she loses her grip, sending her body splashing downward, sliding toward the front of the tub. Her head dips under the water and hits against the bottom. She thrashes out, her hands clawing at something, anything. She grabs the edge, pulling herself up with all her strength. She catapults over the side of the tub. The water spills with her as she strikes the cold tiled floor. She lies on her side, coughing and sputtering for a moment. She wants to scream for her dad, but can't find the breath to do it.

What happened? How could—? Her mind was tangled with the irrationality of what had happened. It couldn't happen again. Not like this. Not in the exact same way.

On unsteady legs she stands—panic squeezes a cold hand on her heart. She's fallen through time again. She's in another Fawlt Line, where no one knows her, where they think she's out of her mind. It's the nightmare all over again.

She throws open the door connecting to her bedroom and stumbles in. Her heart is racing.

The bedroom is dark.

Light spills in from the bathroom. It's her only guide as she makes her way in. Everything is silent, except the sound of her own rabbitlike breathing. Then she hears it. The soft whir of an electric wheelchair. It's coming toward her . . . closer . . . closer . . .

"I know who you are," a soft voice whispers.

Elizabeth cried out.

A flash of light pulled her out of her nightmare and into the arms of her mother. Jane Forde sat on the edge of the bed and wrapped her daughter up in long arms wrapped like angel's wings in a bathrobe. "It's all right," she said softly. "It's all right."

Elizabeth buried her face in her mother's neck.

After a moment, Mrs. Forde relaxed her grip. Elizabeth pulled away and sat up. A tissue materialized out of nowhere, handed over for her wet eyes and dripping nose. "Can you talk about it?" her mother asked.

Elizabeth took a deep, nervous breath. "I was in the bathtub . . . in the other time again."

Her mother frowned. "I'm sorry."

"When I came out, everything was dark. Then I heard it— the wheelchair. And I saw him. The man from the retirement center." Elizabeth had told her parents about him at dinner. "It was awful."

"I'm sure it was."

"I don't know what's wrong with me," she said as she rested her elbows on her knees.

Mrs. Forde clicked her tongue. "There's nothing wrong with you. You're wrung out, that's all. It's understandable. The man— what's his name?"

"George Betterman."

"Well, he makes you uneasy, so he's still on your mind. I'm not surprised you had a dream about him."

"He spoke to me again. He said he knows me." Elizabeth shivered.

Mrs. Forde placed a comforting hand on Elizabeth's. "He's probably a senile old man who doesn't realize what he's saying."

Elizabeth knotted the tissue up. "I don't want to work there anymore."

"I don't blame you."

"You don't?" said Elizabeth, surprised.

"Of course not. It's a new job, and something has brought back all the memories about that other time. And Mr. Creepy-in-a-Wheelchair isn't helping matters."

Elizabeth smiled.

"Look, I know it's not the same," Mrs. Forde continued, "but I remember when I was a cashier in a grocery store. I used to have nightmares about long lines of customers stretching back for miles and, sure enough, someone brought something to the counter without a price tag. Or the bargain was three for fifty-seven cents, and they only brought two. And my manager kept pointing at his watch and saying I had to hurry because the store was closing in two minutes. Talk about nightmares! I'll take Mr. Creepy over those dreams any day!"

Elizabeth laughed, and Mrs. Forde took her hand. "Quitting or not is your decision. But I hope you won't let a nightmare make the decision for you. Give it one more day, just to see what happens."

Elizabeth thought for a moment. One more day. It was a fair proposition. "Okay."

Her mother kissed her on the cheek, and Elizabeth lay back in her bed.

Tucking her in, Mrs. Forde said, "To this day, I don't understand how we almost lost you to that other time. Your father tries to explain it, but I guess I'm too simple-minded."

"You're not simple-minded, Mom. And even Dad is only guessing. Nobody really knows."

"All right, maybe I don't *want to* understand, then. All I know is that I lost you and then I got you back. For that, I will thank God every day as long as I have breath to do it." She kissed her daughter again.

"Good night, Mom."

"Good night." Mrs. Forde floated out of the room on the wings of her housecoat.

Elizabeth lay on her back, staring at the shaft of light that stretched across her ceiling from the hallway. It reminded her of a golden sword.

I lost you and then I got you back. For that, I thank God, her mother had said.

God, don't ever let me get lost like that again, Elizabeth whispered, her fervent "amen" to her mother's statement.

She drifted to sleep as a storm rolled in.

Elizabeth was called to Mrs. Kottler's office as soon as she walked into the retirement center the next afternoon.

"Is something wrong?" she asked Mrs. Spriggins, the purple-haired woman who sat guard at the small wooden desk in the reception area.

"It's the storm," she answered, gesturing to the rain outside. "Something always happens when it rains like this. Two weeks ago it rained and rained, and Grace Peckinpah broke her hip."

Elizabeth didn't understand the connection between the rain, Grace Peckinpah's hip, and Mrs. Kottler's summons. But figuring that she wouldn't find out from Mrs. Spriggins, she walked through the small outer office to Mrs. Kottler's door. The voices on the other side were loud and unmistakable.

"We'll check into it, I promise," Mrs. Kottler said.

"*Who'll* check into it?" Sheriff Hounslow demanded. "Are you telling me you have an investigator on staff?"

"Well, no," Mrs. Kottler stammered. "We'll notify the police."

"I *am* the police!" the sheriff cried.

"Richard, calm down," Adam Hounslow said irritably. "Let me handle this, Dad."

"I know what you're thinking," Mrs. Kottler began in her trademark fashion. "But, Sheriff, they probably weren't stolen at all. Sometimes things are accidentally misplaced."

"She's right. I just forgot where I put them," Adam growled.

"That's nonsense, and you know it, Dad. You're not some senile crackpot—"

"Not yet, but maybe I'm becoming one."

Elizabeth suddenly realized that she was eavesdropping. Glancing back at Mrs. Spriggins, who peered at her over horn-rimmed reading glasses, she knocked softly on the door.

"Come in," Mrs. Kottler said, and looked visibly relieved

when Elizabeth opened the door. "Oh, Elizabeth. I'm so glad you're here."

"Hi," Elizabeth said with a half smile. Mrs. Kottler and Sheriff Hounslow were standing in the center of the office. Adam Hounslow sat on the guest sofa nearby.

"When you were making the rounds with the water yesterday, did you happen to notice a gold ring and an old-fashioned shaving kit, or a framed black-and-white photo anywhere odd?" Mrs. Kottler asked.

"No, ma'am."

"Did you see them on the night stand in my father's room?" Sheriff Hounslow cut in.

"I didn't go into your father's room."

The sheriff frowned. "I saw you there with your tray. Remember? You jumped like you'd seen a ghost."

"But I never went in. I—"

Adam waved a hand at the sheriff. "Leave the poor girl alone."

"Sheriff, I can assure you that our staff and residents are above reproach," Mrs. Kottler said.

"I'm only pointing out that she looked awfully nervous for someone who was just delivering water," Hounslow said defensively.

"It was her first day on the job," Mrs. Kottler said. "Volunteers are always nervous, whether they're delivering water or sweeping the floor."

Elizabeth was grateful for her intercession.

The sheriff folded his arms, which somehow made him look even more of a giant than he was. "Look, Mrs. Kottler, I don't care if these things were accidentally misplaced, stolen, or carried away by fairies in the night. I just want them found. These things were treasures. My mother gave my dad that ring, and the shaving kit was handed down from his father. The photo was his wedding picture."

"Were they your treasures or mine?" Adam demanded.

"Why are you making such a fuss about my things?"

"Because they were valuable!"

Adam's voice was unmistakably mocking. "But they were just things, Richard. Things. And if there's one thing you've taught me, it's that *things* don't last. Like my house."

"Here we go again."

"Was my house misplaced? No, it was stolen from me. Stolen by my own son so he could hide me away in this expensive crypt." Adam sank into the sofa and pouted.

"Stop it!" the sheriff snapped, then turned to Mrs. Kottler. "Maybe I should do a room-by-room search."

Mrs. Kottler shook her head. "That would be terribly stressful for our residents."

"Then what am I supposed to do?"

She spread her hands in appeal. "Let us handle it, Sheriff. We'll look for the missing items. They're bound to turn up."

"Sure they will," he said with obvious disbelief.

"Quit being such a pompous pain in the neck!" Adam snarled. "If you're in such a mood to investigate, why don't you investigate what went wrong with our relationship, huh?"

"That'll be all, Elizabeth. You can go," Mrs. Kottler said with an expression that told Elizabeth she wished she could leave with her.

Elizabeth pulled the door closed on the argument, nodded at Mrs. Spriggins, and went out the door. In the lobby she saw George Betterman whispering to another older man. They stopped as soon as they saw her.

"Good afternoon," she squeaked awkwardly.

The other man waved from his chair. "Afternoon."

George Betterman simply nodded.

Without betraying her desire to run down the hall, Elizabeth walked quickly away. She'd have given anything to just walk out the front door and not come back, but she'd promised her mother—and herself—to give it one more day. Maybe a visit with Frieda Schultz would cheer her up.

The resident's door was open, so Elizabeth peeked in. Frieda was in her bed, propped up against a mountain of pillows. She looked pale and tired, and was staring at a pot of large, pink bell-shaped flowers on the stand next to her.

"Hello, Mrs. Schultz," Elizabeth said as she entered the room.

Frieda jumped. "What do you want?" she cried out before she realized who it was. "Oh, I'm sorry. I didn't know it was you."

"I didn't mean to scare you." Elizabeth smiled.

"Scare me? Ha," Frieda replied with forced humor. "I thought we scared you. I didn't think you'd come back."

Elizabeth was struck by Frieda's worried expression. "Maybe today will be my last day. Unless you can talk me into staying," Elizabeth said playfully.

"I wouldn't try," Frieda said with an unusually serious tone in her voice. "You're young. You should be with the young. Go away from here and don't look back."

Elizabeth stared at her. "What does that mean?"

"Did you happen to bring me water today? My flowers need fresh water," she said, ignoring the question.

"I can get you some," Elizabeth offered and went into the bathroom to fill a glass. "Why are you in bed? Aren't you feeling well?"

"A little tired. And my ankles . . . you know."

"I thought your ankles were just an excuse." Elizabeth returned with a glass of water and came around the bed.

"Not today. Today I need to stay in bed. Just pour it around the edges. Yes, yes, like that. Don't get water on the leaves. Thank you."

"That plant is beautiful. What is it?"

"Don't you know? It's a gloxinia."

"I've never heard of it," Elizabeth said. "My dad loves to work in the garden. Maybe he'll grow some for me."

"Hand me that pad of paper—there, on the dresser—and I'll write the name down for you."

Elizabeth handed her the pad and a pen lettered "Courtesy of Fawlt Line Bank." Frieda's hand trembled slightly as she wrote. Elizabeth adjusted the pot on the table, pushing aside the small prescription bottle and reading glasses next to it. She picked up the prescription bottle. "What're these for?"

"My ankles." Frieda shoved the piece of paper into Elizabeth's uniform pocket. "That'll tell you what you need to know about the flowers."

At that moment, Elizabeth looked Frieda fully in the eyes. The older woman's expression seemed desperate, as if she were trying to communicate something her words weren't saying.

"Mrs. Schultz—"

"Be careful," the old woman whispered.

Elizabeth looked at her quizzically.

"Sshh. It isn't safe. Don't talk." Frieda waved a hand at her as Doug Hall appeared in the doorway.

"My two favorites!" he exclaimed as he walked in. "I knew I'd find you together. Beauty attracts beauty, I always figure."

Elizabeth blushed, and Frieda waved a finger at him. "You're the kind of boy my mother warned me about," she said playfully, but her heart wasn't in it.

"Your mother would have loved me," Doug said with a grin.

Frieda sighed. "Yes. She would have."

Doug looked at Elizabeth. "Mrs. Kottler wants you for sheet detail."

"Sheet detail?"

"Uh-huh. You take the clean sheets from the laundry room and stack them in the various linen closets," he said. "Exciting, huh? I'd rather have you help me in the hot tub, but Mrs. K won't cooperate. How about you, Frieda? Care for some splashing around in the hot tub?"

"It's raining," she said, smiling wearily. "We'd get wet."

"That's the point," he said, and with a Groucho Marx wiggle of his eyebrows he left as suddenly as he'd arrived.

Elizabeth leaned closer to Frieda. "I'll stop by after I finish sheet detail. I want to ask your advice about something."

Frieda nodded.

"Meanwhile, get some rest."

"I think I'll skip the evening recreation time." The older woman gestured to a book on the table. "It'll give me a chance to catch up on my reading."

"Why did you say to be careful?" Elizabeth whispered.

Frieda's eyes darted quickly to the door, and she shook her head. "No, we can't talk. Come back later."

Many of the residents were making their way to the recreation room as Elizabeth wove her way past them to the laundry room. A cart, piled high with cleaned and folded sheets, waited for her.

A short, dark-haired woman stood by the machines at the other end of the room. "Are you the new volunteer?"

"Yes, I'm Elizabeth."

"Terrific," the woman said without meaning it. "I'm Carmel. I'm in charge of the laundry. Now, there are three linen closets around the building. Divide these sheets equally among them, and put 'em *neatly* on the shelves."

"Yes, ma'am," Elizabeth said and, with a hard push, got the cart moving toward the door.

"And don't mix the pillow cases in between them!" the woman shouted. "You volunteers always get 'em mixed up."

"Yes, ma'am," Elizabeth called over her shoulder. She pushed the cart to the first linen closet she came to, around the corner from the recreation room. Music echoed down the hall. A *concert? A dance? Both*, she remembered. Mrs. Kottler had invited in a small ensemble that specialized in big-band music. She had seen the announcement for it on the bulletin board. She wished she could be there. She didn't know anything about big-band music, but it had been a long time since she'd danced with anyone. Jeff didn't like to dance to *any* kind of music.

An image of herself and Doug dancing close together flitted

across her mind. She squashed it immediately. Why did she keep flirting with him in her imagination like that? She couldn't account for it.

She pushed the cart into the linen closet and went about her chore of stacking the sheets in their appropriate places on the large metallic shelves. She was extra careful not to mix in any pillow cases. Ten minutes later she was on her way to the second linen closet, and seven minutes after that she was on her way to the third closet at the far end of the complex. The music and general commotion from the recreation room were now a distant and muted cacophony.

Elizabeth tried to pull the cart into the small closet, but it wouldn't fit. She pushed it back into the hallway. The door bumped into her as it tried to close automatically. Grumbling, she shoved it open again and grabbed a stack of sheets. She wasn't far from Frieda's room. If she hurried and finished the sheet detail, she could visit her again before the recreation time was over.

She stepped halfway into the closet to unload the stack of sheets and froze. She thought she heard something. Was it? *Yes*. The whirring of an electric motor on a wheelchair. The door thumped her from behind again, and the whirring sound came closer. Elizabeth's heartbeat quickened. She didn't want to see George Betterman, and more particularly didn't want to have an encounter with him in a deserted part of the building. She didn't care if her fear was irrational. She didn't care if she had no legitimate reason not to like the man. She moved out of the door's path to let it close. Clutching the sheets, she waited.

The whirring got louder and louder until it was just outside the door. It slowed. Elizabeth pressed her mouth against the sheets. A second passed like an hour. The whirring geared up again and faded away in the opposite direction down the hall.

Elizabeth exhaled long and hard. Her heart banged against her rib cage. She tossed the sheets onto the shelf—still careful not to mix them with the pillowcases—and reached for the closet door handle.

It didn't open.

She pulled at it once, twice, frantically, over and over until her arms and shoulders ached. The door wouldn't budge.

She was locked in.

CHAPTER 6

Elizabeth stood still, her breath wheezing in her ears. Then she renewed her attack on the door, pounding and shouting in the hope that someone *wasn't* in the recreation room and would hear her. How long before someone would come by? Would anyone notice that she was missing? Doug Hall might, if he ran out of other people to flirt with. Maybe Mrs. Kottler would. But today was the big-band concert, and the program would surely go longer than usual.

She leaned against the door and tried to control the panic that threatened to overwhelm her. There was nothing to be afraid of. All she had to do was just sit down and wait until everyone returned from the concert. How long could it really be? An hour, tops. If she had a book she wouldn't complain. It was an hour of her volunteer obligation spent relaxing.

But she couldn't relax. She paced back and forth in the tiny cell. What if they didn't come back for two hours, or even three? What if there were a fire? What if . . . what if . . . what if this were another time fault and, when she stepped through that door, she found herself in another Fawlt Line once again?

Elizabeth swallowed hard. Was it hot in here? Why was she perspiring so?

"Calm down," she said aloud. "You're being really childish. They'll find you in no time at all. And you definitely don't want to look panicked when they do."

She dropped part of the stack of sheets onto the floor and sat down. *Make yourself at home. Be calm.*

Then the wailing started. It was soft at first and sounded as if a lone oboe was playing a solitary, mournful note in the hallway. Elizabeth had heard wind sound like that on cold winter nights. It was ghostlike, haunting. She stood up and rubbed her arms to keep her skin from crawling. The sound got louder. It was unmistakably human. Someone was crying. Not in short sobs, but in a long howl. Where was it coming from? There—that small vent near the top of the wall. But it could've been coming from anywhere or everywhere. It went on and on.

I can't stand it! she cried out and put her hands over her ears. *Somebody make it stop!*

She threw herself at the door again, pounding and screaming for help.

The wail had stopped before she realized it. She listened to the silence, then sat down and wept.

Suddenly, from beyond the closet door, another kind of commotion began. Heavy footsteps—a lot of them—were coming down the hallway. She heard the voices of men and women shouting. Elizabeth leapt to her feet again and renewed her assault on the door, praying to get someone's attention.

Someone jiggled the door handle.

"It's stuck!" she called out. "Can you hear me?"

Something very large was thrown against the door again and again. Elizabeth stepped as far back as possible. The door was defiant at first, then wrenched free as Doug Hall crashed through.

"Doug!" Elizabeth cried and fell into his arms with a sob.

"It's all right," he said soothingly. "That blasted door sticks sometimes. We should have warned you."

With strong hands he grabbed her by the shoulders and looked into her eyes.

"I'm sorry. I'm a big baby," she mumbled.

"Don't worry. Are you really all right?" He guided her out of the closet with his arm around her shoulder.

She nodded, then noticed that some of the medical staff were gathered in a doorway further down the hall.

Doug turned her to face him. Certain he had her attention, he said, "I need to leave you. We have an emergency."

"What's wrong?"

"Frieda Schultz just had a heart attack."

Elizabeth was no stranger to the idea of death. Like many fifteen year olds, she had lost a relative or two and been to a couple of funerals. And she'd almost met death face-to-face at the old saw-mill in the *other* Fawlt Line. But none of those things had prepared her for the overwhelming loss she felt when Frieda Schultz died five minutes later.

She slumped against the wall and poured out whatever tears were left from her trauma in the closet. A moment later, Doug's strong hands were guiding her again, this time to a cozy gathering of chairs at the end of the hall. She didn't resist, even when he sat her down and put his arm around her.

His face was close to hers when he finally spoke. "It's terrible. The poor old girl. She couldn't reach her buzzer to let anyone know."

Elizabeth suddenly remembered the wailing. "Oh, Doug! I heard her when I was in the closet. She was crying. I could have helped her." She broke down again.

"You couldn't have done anything for her," he assured her. "Don't torture yourself. Her heart was bad—did you know that?"

Elizabeth shook her head.

"She didn't like to talk about it. I think she diverted attention from her heart by blaming her ankles or her toes or something."

"Her ankles. She said she had bad ankles," Elizabeth sniffled.

"That's it. There was nothing wrong with her ankles." Doug sighed. "I guess she'd left her pills in the bathroom. Why would she do that? She was supposed to keep them next to her bed."

Elizabeth was too grief-stricken to think about it.

Doug sat silently, then looked at her and said, "I'm going to miss her. She was one of the best things about this place . . . until you came along."

Elizabeth glanced at him. She opened her mouth to speak,

43

but his little compliment moved her, and she started to cry again.

He held her close, gently patting her back. "That's it. Just let it all out. You've had a tough night."

"I hate it here. I never want to come back again," Elizabeth sobbed.

"I feel that way, too, most of the time," Doug said. "Maybe we should get out of here now. Go for a Coke or some ice cream. It'll take our minds off everything."

Elizabeth was tempted. It would be easy to rationalize leaving for a while, considering everything she'd been through.

Doug put a finger under her chin and tipped her face upward. "Let's go crazy and drive up to Hancock. That's where the fun is. I never hang around Fawlt Line unless I have to. How about it?"

"I can't. Jeff is picking me up tonight."

He dismissed the comment. "Who's Jeff—your brother? Call him and tell him you made other plans."

"No," she answered. "He's not my brother. But . . . I really can't, Doug. Thanks for asking."

Doug put on an exaggerated pout. "Okay. I'll let you off this time. But only if you promise to go with me another night."

Elizabeth wanted to say she couldn't because Jeff was her boyfriend. She wanted to say that she was only fifteen years old. But somehow the words wouldn't come. "We'll see," she said noncommittally.

Mrs. Kottler was at their side before either of them realized it. "A tragedy. A real tragedy," she said. "Doug, we're going to need your help with—" She paused to find the right words. "—Certain details."

Doug stood up. "You've got it."

"You look awful, Elizabeth. I can't have you wandering around depressing the residents. Why don't you go on home?"

Mrs. Kottler raced away, and Doug put a hand gently on Elizabeth's shoulder. "Just let me know if you need anything. I got good grades in comforting when I was in school."

She smiled gratefully at him, then got to her unsteady feet. The attendants were wheeling Mrs. Schultz out on a stretcher. Elizabeth could smell her delicate perfume. She stood perfectly still, breathing it in until she could smell it no more.

Further beyond, George Betterman sat alone in the hallway and watched the proceedings. Elizabeth wasn't certain, but she thought she saw a hint of a smile on his face.

CHAPTER 8

Later, the rain stopped and the skies cleared enough for the stars to peek through. Elizabeth and Jeff strolled hand in hand down the freshly paved sidewalks in the Historical Village. Uncle Malcolm had designed it to be as woodsy and parklike as possible.

Jeff hoped a walk would help Elizabeth's mood. She'd been very quiet since he'd picked her up at the center, but he didn't press to find out what was wrong. He knew she'd tell him when she was ready.

"Everything's on schedule for the Village to open," he said finally, just to break the silence.

Elizabeth didn't respond.

Undaunted, Jeff continued, "Uncle Malcolm finalized the deal on the Winchester Estate. It's a perfect replica of a—"

"I don't care, Jeff," Elizabeth said suddenly. "I just wish this Village would hurry up and open, so we could talk about something else for a while."

Jeff was stung, but he didn't show it. "What else do you want to talk about?" he asked.

"Anything."

"Ummm . . . okay. You start."

She frowned. "I don't have anything to say."

"Something's on your mind, Bits."

"I have a *lot* on my mind," she growled.

"Like?"

"Like, why don't we ever go out? I don't mean down to the Fawlt Line Diner. I mean, to Hancock or Grantsville. Just for a change. Don't you ever get tired of hanging around here?"

Jeff was taken by surprise. "What's wrong, Bits? I mean, what's *really* wrong?"

"Nothing's wrong." She frowned. "Why does something have to be wrong for me to want to do something different?"

"Because the last time you talked like this was when you

wanted to run away from home. Remember? Right before—"

"I don't want to talk about that."

They walked on in silence for a moment, then veered down a solitary path. Jeff glanced at the signpost to be sure he knew where they were headed. "Did something happen at the center?"

Elizabeth didn't answer at first, then she took a deep breath. "Mrs. Schultz died of a heart attack."

"Mrs. Schultz? That woman you liked? Oh, Bits, I'm sorry. That's terrible."

It all poured out. "I saw her a little while before. I knew something was wrong. She looked sick and was worried about something when she showed me her flowers."

Jeff cocked an eyebrow. "Worried about what?"

"I don't know. She told me to be careful. I was supposed to go back later to talk to her, but I got locked in the closet and that's when she died."

Jeff shook his head. "Locked in a closet? Good grief, what kind of day did you have?"

Elizabeth told him about the closet and the wailing. "I was locked in that stupid closet while Mrs. Schultz was dying. And what makes it worse is that her pills were right there in the—"

She suddenly stopped and looked puzzled.

"What's wrong?" Jeff asked. "The pills were right where?"

"Wait a minute. That doesn't make sense."

In the dim light Jeff could see that Elizabeth's brow was furrowed in deep thought. "What doesn't make sense?" he asked.

"Her pills. They were on the table with the flowers. I saw them," she said, then thought about it more. "But Doug said that she couldn't get to them because she'd left them in the bathroom. That's not right."

"Are you sure?"

"Yes! They were right next to the flowers. How did they get into the bathroom?"

"Beats me." Jeff shrugged. "Maybe she took them in herself and forgot."

"Or maybe somebody else moved them."

"Why would anybody do that?"

Elizabeth folded her arms. "I don't know. But something's not right."

"Bits," Jeff said with a hint of impatience, "I'm not following you."

"George Betterman," she said.

"Huh? The guy in the wheelchair?"

"He's the reason I got stuck in the closet. I heard him coming, and I didn't want him to see me, so I let the door close. That's when it got stuck."

"I still don't understand what that has to do with—"

"Don't you see? He was coming from Mrs. Schultz's room!"

Jeff stopped abruptly on the path and turned to her. "Wait a minute. Are you saying George Betterman took Mrs. Schultz's pills?"

"Maybe."

Jeff bit his lower lip. "But that's the same as saying he killed her."

Elizabeth nodded and walked on down the path.

Jeff followed. "Do you really think Mrs. Schultz was murdered?"

"I don't know!" Elizabeth cried. "That's the problem! Nothing makes sense. He keeps looking at me and giving me nightmares—"

"Nightmares?" Jeff asked, feeling more lost with every question he asked.

"Last night. I was going to quit the retirement center because of it. I was trapped in the other time again, and I walked into my room and *he* was there. For some reason, he reminds me of that other time. He brings back all the worst fears I have."

Jeff pulled her close. "The chances are really slim—almost nonexistent—that you'll ever go back there. Uncle Malcolm said so."

"How does he know that? Nobody knows. Freak coincidences happen all the time around here."

Jeff wagged a finger at her in mock rebuke. "Remember what

Charles Richards said. 'Coincidences are the secret workings of God.' "

"Yeah—and Charles is still stuck there!" Her voice was a shrill contrast to the peacefulness of the evening.

"Calm down, Bits. It's okay."

"I wish I could go through and save him like he saved me!" she said.

Jeff steered her toward a bench, and they sat down. He gently caressed her hair. "You can't get back anyway. Why torment yourself? You know how exact everything has to be on both sides of time for anyone to cross over. You and Sarah would have to be in the right places at the right times . . . and the chances of that must be a trillion to one. It won't happen again. You're safe."

"And Charles is trapped."

"I guess he is," Jeff said simply, but not without sympathy.

She glanced up and realized they were sitting across from the church ruin. It was a restored section of a church from England where, through a different time fault, King Arthur had slipped through into the present. Its towers and vaulted ceilings stood over them majestically.

"What about that?" Elizabeth asked. "King Arthur didn't switch places with anyone. He just came through."

"He came through for a specific reason and—" Jeff turned to her impatiently. "Look, I didn't say I had the answers for everything. All I know is what Uncle Malcolm says. Eternity is . . . well, it's like a very large house and . . . somewhere inside the house is a hallway that we call time. Maybe that hallway has different doors that are usually closed,
but sometimes they slip open. Why they open and what happens when they do is anybody's guess. Only God knows for sure.
All I know for sure is that we have our time right here and now, and we shouldn't waste it by worrying about things we don't understand."

He pulled Elizabeth close and kissed her.

"But what am I going to do about the retirement center?" she whispered.

"Do you want to quit?"

"Yes."

"Then quit. Tell them tomorrow. That way you can forget about that guy in the wheelchair and Mrs. Schultz and everyone else."

"What about Mrs. Schultz's pills?"

Jeff shrugged. "You could tell Sheriff Hounslow. You see a lot of him these days."

"He'd never believe me."

"Maybe not. But it won't hurt to try."

CHAPTER 9

"Gone? What do you mean, she's gone?" Elizabeth asked.

Mrs. Kottler smiled indulgently from behind her desk. "That's the procedure. She's examined to determine the cause of death, and then she'll be transported to her family in—" she flipped over a form on her desk to check her information "—New York City."

"That's it? I won't get to see her again?"

"I'm sorry. I didn't realize you'd become so fond of her," Mrs. Kottler said, rising from her chair and quickly moving around the desk.

"I thought I'd have a chance to say good-bye," Elizabeth said calmly.

Mrs. Kottler patted Elizabeth's arm. "In your own way, I'm sure you still can."

Elizabeth sighed.

"I know what you're thinking," Mrs. Kottler said. "You're thinking that this will hurt the morale of the rest of the residents. But your friend Malcolm Dubbs has helped to allay that problem."

"He has?"

She smiled. "Oh yes! The whole building is abuzz. He has generously extended an offer for all the residents to come to the grand opening of the Historical Village for free!"

Elizabeth was impressed. "That's nice of him."

"Everyone is so delighted, and I can't say enough about his generosity! Even Adam Hounslow seems uncharacteristically pleased."

Elizabeth was even more impressed, and then remembered about Mrs. Schultz's pills. "Has the sheriff come in to see his father today?"

"Not yet. He doesn't usually arrive until around dinner time. Why?"

"I was just wondering."

Mrs. Kottler scrutinized Elizabeth carefully. "Are you all right? I'm sure what happened yesterday was a shock for you. Doug told me about your being locked in the closet. And then Mrs. Schultz dying . . . I'm certain you must be thinking about resigning."

"To be honest—"

"Oh, I hope you won't!" Mrs. Kottler exclaimed. "We're so desperate for help, and having young people around does wonders for our residents. You have no idea! You're all they've been talking about. The 'fresh-faced young girl,' they call you. Just seeing you makes them feel younger and more alive."

Except for Mrs. Schultz, Elizabeth thought bleakly.

A mischievous smile formed on Mrs. Kottler's lips. "Doug Hall would be devastated if you left now. Please promise me that you won't make any decision based on what happened yesterday."

It suddenly occurred to Elizabeth that if some kind of foul play was responsible for Mrs. Schultz's death, maybe she could help expose it by sticking around. *But only if I can stay at opposite ends of the universe from George Betterman*, she thought. Elizabeth didn't promise anything to Mrs. Kottler, but she cautiously nodded her consent.

"Excellent!" Mrs. Kottler cried out and hugged Elizabeth gingerly, so as not to wrinkle their outfits. She briskly set about organizing Elizabeth's role in preparing the recreation room for the evening craft class. "Simply arrange the tables and chairs so that everyone can see the front clearly. Well, as clearly as most of them can see anything."

Alone in the room, Elizabeth began the tedious process of moving chairs. Doug showed up a few minutes later and looked surprised to see her. "I just lost five dollars in the betting pool," he announced. "Everyone was debating whether you'd be back. I see I didn't have enough faith in your strength of character."

Elizabeth blushed. "I would've bet against my coming back, too," she confessed.

He grabbed some chairs to help her rearrange the room. "Really? Then why did you? My godlike good looks, right?"

She giggled. "Actually, it was Adam Hounslow's good looks."

"I should've pegged you for one of those women who like the old, wizened types." He scowled playfully, then his tone became softer. "I meant what I said about going out. I'd like to get to know you better."

"I'm only fifteen," she protested.

"So am I!" he lied. "We were made for each other."

Elizabeth rested her hands on one of the folding tables and rocked nervously. "Look, Doug, I . . . I didn't say so yesterday, but . . . I have a boyfriend."

Doug feigned great shock. "You do?" he gasped.

"His name is Jeff. I think you'd like him."

"I hate him already," Doug said good-naturedly. In mock anger he pushed over a chair, and it crashed to the floor with a loud metallic clang.

"Everything all right in here?" Sheriff Hounslow asked from the doorway.

Startled, Elizabeth jumped, then put a hand over her mouth to stifle a giggle.

"Everything's fine, Sheriff," Doug said quickly as he scooped up the chair.

"I'm looking for Mrs. Kottler," the sheriff said sharply. "Do you know where she is?"

"No sir," Doug replied. Elizabeth shook her head to confirm his reply.

"I'll assume that, since we haven't heard otherwise, no one has found my father's belongings?"

Doug took a few steps toward the sheriff, presumably to keep from shouting their entire conversation. "I'm sorry, no. But we're sure they'll turn up."

"Uh-huh," the sheriff said skeptically and moved to retreat.

"Sheriff!" Elizabeth suddenly called out. She wanted to talk to him about Mrs. Schultz and the pills.

"Yeah?"

She opened her mouth to speak, but felt uncomfortable mentioning it in front of Doug. "Are you taking your father to the Village for the grand opening tomorrow?" she asked instead.

Hounslow grimaced. "I hadn't planned on it, but my dad seems to be excited about the idea. I can't imagine why."

"Why did you people ever elect him sheriff?" Doug asked, as Hounslow walked away.

Elizabeth shrugged. "Don't look at me. I'm too young to vote."

Later, during her evening break, Elizabeth stopped by Frieda Schultz's room. Someone had been busy. Most of Frieda's belongings were boxed up for shipping. The bed was stripped, the wardrobe doors stood open to reveal their emptiness, all surfaces were bare except for the night stand. Frieda's flowers still sat there in their pot looking beautiful, oblivious to the loss of their owner. The room looked like any other hospital room now. Even the smell of her perfume was gone.

Good-bye, Elizabeth thought. In the silence of the room, she remembered a phrase she'd heard at her Great-aunt Patricia's funeral: *Have mercy on your servant and commend her to everlasting peace.*

"Amen," she whispered aloud.

No sooner had she finished her prayer than she heard the whirring of an electric wheelchair. Elizabeth's ears were attuned to it now. She reacted quickly by moving around the bed and into the darkness of the bathroom, glancing warily at the door as she entered. If this one closed and locked her in, she might lose her mind.

She listened as the whirring approached the room. *Please let it pass,* she prayed, but it didn't. It came into the room.

George Betterman paused at the door, tipping his head ever so slightly this way and that in an almost mechanical way. Was he making sure the room was empty? Elizabeth put both hands over her mouth and tightened every muscle in her body to keep from moving—or shaking.

He guided the wheelchair past the bed and wove around the packed boxes.

What's he doing here? Elizabeth wondered. *What's he want? Maybe he's checking for evidence, to make sure he didn't leave anything behind.*

He came to the night stand and looked at the flowers. Leaning forward, he pushed his nose into the bouquet and inhaled deeply.

Without realizing it, Elizabeth pressed against the sink. The porcelain clicked loudly. Elizabeth's heart skipped a beat, and she stepped further into the darkness.

Again George Betterman tipped his head this way and that, then gently picked up the pot and put it on his lap. He grabbed the controls to the wheelchair and spun himself around. Elizabeth closed her eyes. Her mouth had gone dry. She desperately wanted to swallow, but feared the sound it might make.

The angle from the bathroom to the door gave her a clear view of him again—and him of her, if he happened to turn to look. She began to relax as he moved steadily toward the hallway.

Just before he reached the door, he stopped his wheelchair. He didn't look at her, but Elizabeth knew he was speaking to her anyway. "It'd be a shame for these flowers to die," he said. "I think it's a shame for *anyone* to die."

Elizabeth froze. She didn't breathe.

Then he did turn his head to face her. His black glasses reflected the fluorescent lights above in a way that made them look like lightning. "Wouldn't you agree, *Sarah*?"

"He called you Sarah?!" Jeff shouted.

Malcolm waved at him. "Sit down and be quiet, Jeff. Can't you see she's upset enough?"

Elizabeth was sitting on the sofa in Malcolm's study. She'd

called Jeff immediately to come pick her up at the center, but she didn't tell him what had happened until they were together with Uncle Malcolm.

Jeff sat down next to her. "I'm sorry, Bits. It'll be okay. Maybe it's just a . . . a name to him. Someone else's name."

"A coincidence?" Malcolm challenged him. "Is that what you're saying?"

"Maybe," Jeff answered sheepishly. "How could he know? We never talked to anyone about what happened in the other Fawlt Line. Apart from us and Bits's parents, nobody knows the whole story. Nobody else knows that the girl you swapped places with was named Sarah."

"I told Sheriff Hounslow," Malcolm remembered.

"But he didn't believe you," Jeff replied. "And for Elizabeth's sake, he promised not to talk about it. The last thing any of us wanted was for tabloid reporters to come in and turn Fawlt Line into some kind of freak show. This George Betterman character *must* have made the name up, or has Elizabeth confused with someone he knows."

"I don't think so." Malcolm tugged at his ear. "I wonder what kind of game he's playing."

"It's called the Let's-Scare-Elizabeth-to-Death Game," Elizabeth answered shakily.

Jeff was relieved to see some color returning to her cheeks.

Malcolm paced for a moment with his hands folded behind his back—a sure sign that he was trying to work it all out in his head. "I suppose we could talk to him directly, but I doubt he'd tell us anything. I wonder where he's from. Maybe Mrs. Kottler can tell us something. No, asking her might draw too much attention to the situation. Hmm. What's the best way to proceed?"

"Then you believe me?" Elizabeth asked with a look of gratitude. "You think there's something weird going on at the retirement center?"

"I certainly do," said Malcolm. "There are too many odd connections not to believe you. This Sarah business clinches it."

"But *what* do you think is going on?" Jeff asked, bewildered.

Malcolm looked at Jeff helplessly. "In a million years, I couldn't guess. Not with this little bit of information. We'll have to watch and see."

"Watch and see?" Elizabeth asked. "Oh, no, I'm not going back. I can't. My volunteering days are over."

"You don't have to go back if you don't want to," Malcolm said. "You've done your four days this week. Now you have a few days to relax and put it out of your mind."

"Not a chance."

"Maybe Betterman will come to the grand opening," Malcolm said hopefully. "I might get a chance to see him there."

"And then what?" Jeff asked.

"Then we'll play it as it comes."

CHAPTER 10

Saturday came quickly, and no one could have been more surprised than Elizabeth to find that she really had been able to relax and put the troubles at the retirement center out of her mind in the intervening time.

Under blue skies and a hot sun, people came from all over for the grand opening of the Historical Village. At noon, the mayor made a long speech congratulating Malcolm for his contributions to local economy—as if that were the reason Malcolm built the Village—then, with a pair of gigantic gold scissors, cut a long red ribbon wound around the front gates. Someone on the city council read a telegram offering the best wishes of the governor. Red, white, blue, pink, purple, silver, and gold balloons were released all over the grounds and flew to the clouds like psychedelic geese.

The crowds poured in and, for a little while, the parking attendants and security guards were afraid they'd have to turn people away. Luke Goodwin, the fire marshal, twitched his thick gray mustache and kept a watchful eye. Reporters for newspapers and local television stations spread out and interviewed anyone they could persuade to stop and talk. Even a national news network showed up for five minutes with a reporter and a camera. Malcolm said it must've been a slow news day.

Jeff and Elizabeth strolled the grounds and tried to enjoy the Village with everyone else. It was easy for Elizabeth, since she'd mostly steered clear of the chaos around its organization. Jeff, on the other hand, had helped where he could, doing everything from painting sites to coordinating the delivery of antiques, and was aware of all the things they hadn't been able to finish. But the smile on his face told everyone that he was proud to be Malcolm's nephew.

Near the miners' row-house display in the southwest corner of the Village, Elizabeth spotted some residents from the retirement center. Sheriff Hounslow walked past with his father, bickering as usual. Dolly Higgins, a gnome of a woman with a bright smile and twinkling eyes, tweaked Elizabeth on the cheek and called her the "fresh-faced young girl." Then she looked at Jeff and asked in a singsong voice, "Is this your boyfriend?"

"Yes, he is." Elizabeth smiled back.

Dolly looked Jeff up and down and said, "Oh, I could fancy one of those myself."

Jeff turned crimson, and Elizabeth laughed.

It looked to Elizabeth as though most of the center's residents had come. They wandered in groups of two or three, some with members of the staff or family. Some hobbled along with walkers, some rode in wheelchairs or the carts Malcolm had provided for anyone who needed them. They stared wide-eyed at the nineteenth-century farmhouse, the Shakespearean-style cottage, the Dutch windmill, the church ruin, the cluster of schoolhouses that represented the development of education in the United States throughout the past three centuries, the 1920 gas station, the grocery stores. . . .

As Elizabeth watched some of the residents gather around the twentieth-century displays, she imagined the memories that were surfacing. "Do you remember that?" she heard someone say, and "Oh, we had one of those in our house" or "I used to play in a room like that." Some merely stared wistfully.

What were they thinking? Did they long for a piece of their past, or wish for a time lost to them? Or maybe they reached out with the desire to reclaim what was once theirs—their youth, their happiness, their missing loved ones?

"Look at them," Jeff said softly, and Elizabeth knew he was wondering the same thing. "They make the whole thing worthwhile. It's not just history to them. It's part of their lives."

"Well, now, look at the happy couple," a voice said from behind them.

Elizabeth and Jeff turned to find themselves face-to-face with Doug Hall.

"Doug!" Elizabeth cried. "I didn't know you were coming."

"I wouldn't miss it." He smiled, then stretched out a hand to Jeff. "You must be Jeff. Elizabeth's told me a lot about you."

Jeff shook his hand. "Funny, she didn't mention you at all."

"I'm her little secret at the retirement center." He winked. "I'll bet you thought she was volunteering for humanitarian reasons. Don't believe it."

"Doug rescued me from the closet," Elizabeth explained quickly.

"Oh—that was nice of you," Jeff said.

"I thought so, too." He nodded, then said, "Well, I better go. Mrs. Kottler asked me to play camp counselor for the kids today. Nice to meet you, Jeff." He darted off into a group of residents, and the ladies instantly began cooing over his arrival.

"So," Jeff said as nonchalantly as he could, "how many times has he asked you out?"

Elizabeth giggled evasively and put her arm in his. "Don't be silly. There's nothing to be jealous about."

"I'm not jealous."

Elizabeth changed the subject. "I haven't seen George Betterman."

"Maybe he decided not to come."

"That suits me just fine."

At a fork in the path leading to the miners' row houses in one direction and the Park 'n' Dine Diner in the other, they bumped into Sheriff Hounslow again. He was standing in the middle of the crowd, hand to brow, scanning the area.

"You haven't seen him, have you?" he asked them.

"Who? Your father?" Elizabeth replied. "No."

"You lost your dad, Sheriff?" Jeff teased. "How did you do that?"

The sheriff gave him a cold look. "We were going through the miners' houses when he sent me off to get him a drink." He brandished a cup of soda as if to prove his story. "When I got back, he was gone."

"Maybe you should go to the office or the lost-and-found,"

Jeff offered. "They have speakers set up throughout the village so announcements for lost kids, or lost parents, can be made."

Preoccupied again, the sheriff continued to look through the crowd. "It's confounding," he muttered as he walked away. "It's like he *wanted* to lose me."

"I've had the same feelings myself," Jeff said after he'd gone.

They circled through the Village and made their way toward the front gate again. Both were surprised that it was already late afternoon. They stopped by the front office where Malcolm was giving directions to the parking supervisor via a walkie-talkie. He signed off.

"All in all, the day has been a success," Malcolm said, beaming.

"A huge success, Uncle Malcolm," Elizabeth corrected him.

"No crises, no catastrophes."

Jeff held up a finger. "No, wait. You've had one. Sheriff Hounslow's father has disappeared."

Malcolm looked surprised. "Really? I haven't heard anything about that."

"Don't worry about it. He's bound to turn up soon," Elizabeth said.

Suddenly Mrs. Kottler was upon them. "There you are, Elizabeth. I was wondering when I would bump into you. Oh, hello again, Mr. Dubbs—"

"Malcolm."

"Malcolm, of course," Mrs. Kottler laughed. "And you're Jeff, I know. It's been a wonderful day so far, hasn't it? Thanks ever so much for allowing our residents to come. We're trying to get them back to the center now. You can imagine how tired they are. But—and I'm so embarrassed about this—we seem to have botched up our car pool. Dolly Higgins's family brought her, but they couldn't take her back, so we're one off. Anyway, Dolly needs a ride, and I'm absolutely desperate to come up with how to get her there without making another trip. . . ." She let her final sentence hang for a moment.

Jeff grabbed it. "Elizabeth and I would be happy to help. We can take Dolly back."

Mrs. Kottler flapped her arms excitedly. "Oh, would you? Oh, you're wonderful. Thank you. She's right out here whenever you're ready to go. No rush. She's just outside on the bench. Thank you, thank you!" She left the office with heavy perfume in her slipstream.

Elizabeth tweaked Jeff's cheek. "You're wonderful as well as cute!"

They collected Dolly and walked slowly with her to Jeff's Volkswagen. As they wound their way through the parking lot, Elizabeth spotted Doug Hall also walking between rows of cars. She nearly called out to him until she realized he was pushing a wheelchair. In it was George Betterman.

"That's him," she whispered to Jeff out of Dolly's earshot.

Jeff glanced around quickly. "It looks like they're leaving. Uncle Malcolm will be disappointed that he missed him."

"I'm not."

They reached the edge of the employee parking area where Jeff had left his Beetle earlier in the day. Elizabeth crawled into the back so Dolly would have an easier time getting in. Dolly thanked them at least a dozen times for being so nice to her.

As they putted along to the retirement center, Elizabeth thought about George Betterman and Doug Hall again. *Wait a minute,* she thought. *Why was Doug pushing George's electric wheelchair?*

CHAPTER 11

Jeff waited in the car while Elizabeth walked Dolly to her room. Though it was still early evening, the hallways in the retirement center were fairly deserted.

"Everyone's worn out from such an exciting day," Dolly said when they reached her doorway. "I'm a mite tired myself."

"Me too."

"Thank you for the lift home, dear. Good night." Dolly shuffled into her room.

Elizabeth waved good night and walked back down the hall. She passed Adam Hounslow's room and remembered that he had disappeared earlier in the day. Maybe he got separated from his son and found a way back to his room somehow. She stopped to check, but the door was shut. It was unusual for the residents to close their doors, even when they were away. She knocked softly. No response. She knocked again and whispered, "Mr. Hounslow?" Still no response. She reached down and put her fingers on the door handle.

"What are you doing?" a voice echoed down the hall.

She jumped and turned. George Betterman had been watching her from the end of the corridor. He put his wheelchair into gear and drove toward her. She wanted to run, but was afraid it would make her look guilty of something. "Sheriff Hounslow couldn't find his father at the Village, so I thought I'd check to see if he was here."

"He's not," Betterman said.

"Oh. Okay." Elizabeth turned to leave.

"Sheriff Hounslow's a policeman. If he can't find his father, what makes you think you can?"

Elizabeth felt her face go red. "I didn't say I could find him. I just thought, since I was here, I'd peek in. That's all."

"Well, he's not, Sarah, so don't worry your pretty little head about him."

Elizabeth faced Betterman fully—aware of his trademark jogging outfit and shoes, the cap and beard and mustache, and the black sunglasses that wouldn't let her see his eyes. "Why did you call me Sarah?"

A flicker of a smile formed at the corners of his mouth. "It's your name, isn't it?"

"No," she said. "My name's Elizabeth."

"I'm sure that's what they keep telling you. But we know better, don't we?"

Every instinct in Elizabeth's body told her to get away, and get away now. "I think you have me confused with someone else."

The tiny smile stayed frozen beneath his whiskers. "I'm sure that I don't."

"I have to go," Elizabeth said abruptly and spun around to walk away.

"We'll talk again soon," he laughed.

His laughter was still ringing in her ears when she collapsed into the passenger seat of Jeff's Volkswagen.

"I didn't know you were going to tuck her in and read her a bedtime story," he said.

"Just drive," she snapped.

When Jeff heard about Elizabeth's encounter with George Betterman, he thought it was worth driving back to the Village to tell Uncle Malcolm. The sun was falling when they arrived. The first thing they noticed was the presence of several police cars in the employee lot. Jeff and Elizabeth walked through the front gate, where one of Hounslow's officers eyed them suspiciously. He relaxed when he realized who they were.

"What's going on?" Jeff asked him.

"The sheriff's father is missing. We're watching the gates while the staff search the park."

Jeff and Elizabeth went straight to the office. It was in a state of chaos as stricken-looking staff buzzed around Malcolm and Sheriff Hounslow, waiting for orders. Spread in front of them on the desk was an array of blueprints for places to search.

"I'm telling you, we've turned this place upside down," Deputy Peterson, the sheriff's right-hand man, said. His uniform, badly fitted around his squat, barrel-like body, was damp with sweat. He grabbed a handkerchief and wiped the beads of water off his bald head. "We can check again, but I don't think he's here."

"What's standard procedure in a case like this?" Malcolm asked.

Sheriff Hounslow was pacing nearby. "Standard procedure is to wait twenty-four hours before putting in a missing person's report."

Jeff nodded to Elizabeth. That's what he'd been told when she had vanished.

"We're talking about your *father*, Richard," Malcolm reminded him. "If it were twenty-four hours later, what would we be doing?"

"We'd have to look at the various possibilities," Hounslow said and paused in his pacing to peer out of the office window that overlooked the Village. "Maybe he had a heart attack and collapsed somewhere in the park."

"But we've already—" Deputy Peterson began.

Hounslow held up a hand. "I know, I know. He's not here. So we might consider that the heat of the day affected his mind and he wandered off."

"Has anyone checked the retirement center?" Malcolm asked.

"We were just there," Jeff interjected. "Elizabeth went inside and stopped by his room. They said he wasn't there."

"Who said?" Hounslow asked.

"George Betterman," Elizabeth replied. With the mention of that name, Malcolm looked curiously at Elizabeth, then Jeff. Jeff nodded as if to say they needed to talk later.

"Don't know him. Bob, send someone out to make absolutely sure," the sheriff said.

"Already done," Peterson replied. "Mrs. Kottler is having her people check around."

"Okay, so we fan out from the park to see if he's wandered off in some kind of daze," Malcolm said.

"Yeah," the sheriff said wearily, rubbing the back of his neck. Deputy Peterson grabbed his cap and went out to see that it was done. With the exodus of Peterson and some of the staff, the office was left to Malcolm, the sheriff, Jeff, and Elizabeth.

Hounslow sat down heavily in a chair and spoke as if he'd been in the middle of a thought. "Unless he's been kidnapped."

"Do you think that's likely?" Malcolm asked, surprised.

"No, but I can't rule it out," Hounslow replied. "I'll tell you what's *likely*. He ran away."

"You're kidding."

Hounslow shook his head. "If I treated this like any other case, I'd have to consider it as a possibility. He hated the retirement center. Maybe he came up with a way to escape."

"Escape to where? Does he have other relatives or friends?" Malcolm asked.

"No. Which is why it's hard for me to imagine him actually doing it. But, as I said, I have to consider every possibility." Hounslow sighed.

The four of them waited in silence for a moment. Elizabeth wondered if now was the time to tell the sheriff about the strange things that had been happening at the retirement center. Maybe there was a connection between Frieda Schultz's death and his father's disappearance.

She was just mustering the courage to bring up the subject when Hounslow suddenly leapt to his feet. "I'm not waiting around here. I want to go back to that mining display."

"The row houses?"

"That's the last place I saw him. I might have a better chance of finding a clue now that most of the people have gone."

Until the last half of the twentieth century, coal mining was the most important industry for Fawlt Line and the surrounding towns. New technology and energy sources diminished the need for coal, and one by one the mines closed down. Malcolm wanted to pay tribute to the many people who worked in the mines by recreating the kinds of row houses they lived in over the years.

Sheriff Hounslow, Malcolm, Jeff, and Elizabeth walked into the small row house that represented the late 1920s. It had the kinds of things most homes would have: a small living room with a sofa, chair, and reading lamp sitting on a large worn rug. A coal-burning stove called a "Heatrola" sat in the corner. The walls had a few meager framed photos of stern-looking men and women washed out in sepia tones.

"My father was the son of a miner," Hounslow said as he glanced around the room. "Houses like this were called company houses, because the mining company owned them. The miners nicknamed them 'patches.' My father grew up in one just like it."

The kitchen was visible through an adjacent doorway. They crowded in. A free standing sink and coal-oven range, a small wooden table and several shelves stocked with Campbell's soups, Morton's salt, baking powder, Pillsbury flour, Jack Frost Cane Sugar, Ivory starch, and Borax soap lined one wall. A bathtub with a wooden cover sat along another wall. Several hooks in the wall above it held a large coat, a black mining helmet with a lamp attached to the front, and a hand-held lantern. A lunch pail sat next to a pair of old black shoes on the floor. Elizabeth was struck by the starkness of it all.

Hounslow continued, "My dad used to tell me how his father would come home with a face so black from the coal dust that all you could see were the whites of his eyes. He climbed into one of those old tubs, and the kids would take turns scrubbing the dirt from his back."

Malcolm walked over to a door on the opposite wall and jiggled the door handle.

"Does that go anywhere?" the sheriff asked.

"When we get to phase three or four of this Village, it may

lead to a back garden. But for now there's a wall on the other side."

The four of them squeezed up the narrow flight of stairs to the second floor.

"Did your dad work for the mines, too?" Elizabeth asked.

Hounslow nodded. "Before I was born. But one night there was a cave-in, and his mining partner was killed. He quit right then. But there was something about the mines that stayed in his soul. He talked about them a lot. I think that's why he wanted to see this display so badly. Do you have a company store?"

"Company store?" Jeff asked.

"Department stores for miners," Hounslow replied. "They sold everything from furniture and clothes to shoe polish and matchsticks. But they often took advantage of the miners. Some of the mining companies paid their workers with vouchers that could only be used in the company store, so the miners had no choice but to buy there—and pay twice what they would have paid in regular money at a regular store."

"That's not fair," Elizabeth said.

Hounslow agreed, then pushed open a door on the right side of the upstairs hallway. "Should this be closed?"

"Probably not," Malcolm answered.

The door opened into a bedroom. It had a bed, dresser, wardrobe, and night stand. Near the small window stood a wash table with a small mirror attached to the top. A washing bowl sat on the top center with various toiletries surrounding it.

Suddenly Hounslow's face went pale, and he walked slowly over to the wash table.

"What's wrong?" Malcolm asked.

Sitting at the back of the table was an old black-and-white photo of a man and a woman taken on their wedding day. Next to the photo were an old shaving kit and a modest gold ring.

The sheriff said with choked emotion, "These belong to my father."

CHAPTER 12

Donald Nelson, a meticulous man with a thin face and body that seemed to come to a point at every opportunity, was in his office—a glass-enclosed cage in the corner of the Village's receiving warehouse. As the director of the Village's acquisitions, it was his responsibility to label and catalogue every item placed in the Village, no matter how large or small. As a result, his desk and the surrounding floor looked like a time-traveler's garage sale. There were items ranging from Victorian pen sets to cowboy boots, Napoleonic brooches to eighteenth-century baby cribs, colonial American wigs to Slavic milk wagons.

He peered over his horn-rimmed glasses as Malcolm, Sheriff Hounslow, Elizabeth, and Jeff hurried in. The glow of his desktop computer screen was reflected in his glasses and tinted the two patches of white hair that sprung from above his ears a light green. "Hullo, Malcolm," he said in a high voice. "What are you doing here? You should be out celebrating the success of your grand opening!"

"No more than you, Donald," Malcolm replied, then introduced everyone. "We're still trying to find the sheriff's father. You've heard about him?"

"Missing, right? Yes, some of the staff were in here searching an hour or so ago. It certainly puts a damper on the day."

Careful not to smudge potential fingerprints on the shaving kit, photo, or ring, the sheriff had put them in plastic bags. He now held them up for Donald to look at. "Recognize these?" he asked.

Donald laughed. "As well as I might recognize any of the other thousands of items we have displayed here. No, Sheriff, I'm sorry. But if you'd be so kind as to put them on the desk, I can look for an identifying number and check it against our inventory on the computer. We have complete purchasing histories of everything here."

Hounslow obliged, and Donald looked the items over, humming and cooing as he did. "Very nice." He brought them closer to a red lamp and scrutinized each one through a large magnifying glass. "Your father's, were they?"

"Yeah."

"He took very good care of them," Donald said. "Even the ring is barely scratched."

"Do you recognize them or not?"

Donald didn't seem to notice the sheriff's impatience. "Nothing on any of them that indicates they've been through our system. No numbers, not even the infrared mark. However, even my staff are fallible. Perhaps we missed them. I'll cross-reference the items on the computer." He swung around to the keyboard and hammered in the descriptions. The computer beeped a couple of times, then displayed the information.

"Well?" Hounslow asked.

Donald shook his head. "Very curious. They're not listed. Where exactly did you find them?"

"In the 1920s miners' row house," Malcolm answered.

"I'll check that as well," Donald said. A dozen clickety-clicks later, he frowned. "They're not listed. Whoever brought them in, didn't check them through my office."

Malcolm turned to Hounslow. "Is it possible your father put them there?"

"That's ridiculous," the sheriff replied. "Why would he do a thing like that?"

"Why would he disappear?" Malcolm retorted.

The radio on the sheriff's belt hissed to life with crackle and static. "Sheriff?"

Hounslow grabbed the radio. "Hounslow."

"Nick here, sir," a young voice said. "I'm at the retirement center and, well, you should probably come out here."

"Did you find my father?"

"Not really, but . . ." The rookie didn't finish. "You just oughtta come."

"I'll be right there." Hounslow signed off. He looked at

Donald and struggled with his words. "I'm sorry to be so irritable, but you must understand how anxious I am to find out how my father's things got in that mining house."

Donald nodded gravely. "Sheriff, rest assured I'll keep digging. If there's anything I can find out about your father's things, I'll let you know."

"Thank you." He jabbed a finger toward Malcolm. "We're not finished with this business." He marched off.

Malcolm, Jeff, and Elizabeth looked at each other quizzically. It hadn't occurred to them *not* to be involved in this strange case. All three felt swept along in the mystery and, to some degree and for varying reasons, responsible for its outcome. Elizabeth couldn't shake all the bizarre little events she'd witnessed leading up to Adam's disappearance, and couldn't help but believe there was some sort of connection. Malcolm and Jeff felt possessive enough about the Village's reputation to want to help in any way they could to keep its name cleared.

"Let's go," Malcolm said.

"Wait a minute, Malcolm." Donald beckoned.

Malcolm looked back to Jeff and Elizabeth. "You two go on to the retirement center. Call me later."

Jeff nodded and took Elizabeth by the hand. They strode off through the warehouse to his Volkswagen.

Meanwhile, Donald tapped his computer screen. "There's an entry here—completely mislabeled and misfiled. It looks like the sheriff's father's belongings. One gold ring . . . here's the shaving kit and . . . here's the wedding photo. Miss Clark!"

A pretty blonde-haired girl peeked out from between two large packing crates halfway across the warehouse. "Yes, sir?"

He gestured for her to come. "Miss Clark is a history student who's been interning with us this summer," he explained to Malcolm.

Miss Clark, whose tanned good looks and khaki outfit looked more appropriate for someone hiking on a mountain than inventorying artifacts in a warehouse, arrived at Donald's desk.

"What's the meaning of this?" Donald asked and pointed to the screen.

She squinted at the list. "The meaning of it?"

"This is sloppy work," Donald said without being unkind. "These items shouldn't be under a miscellaneous category."

She ran her fingers through her blonde locks. "I'm sorry. I assume that in the rush of the last few days, someone didn't take the time to catalog those items properly. I'd gladly take the blame, but"—she pointed to the date of the delivery—"I wasn't here that day."

Donald grunted and scrolled down the screen to find out where the delivery had come from. As he did, he dismissed her. "Thank you. But get the word around to the rest of the staff. I won't tolerate shabby procedures."

"Yes, sir," she said and quickly disappeared behind another crate.

"Any idea where they came from?" Malcolm asked.

Donald held up a finger. "Yes. Miller's Olde Antique store, here in our very own Fawlt Line." He grabbed the phone and, using the number listed on the screen, dialed. He asked about their store hours, then hung up. "It closes at nine. We have twenty minutes."

At the retirement center, Mrs. Kottler was beside herself. "Sheriff, I have no idea what happened here," she said.

The sheriff was livid as he stood at the doorway to his father's room.

Jeff and Elizabeth positioned themselves across the hall, but could see into the room clearly. Someone had cleaned it out completely. All that was left was the bed, with its rolled-up mattress, and the institutional night stand and wardrobe.

"It looks as though he was never even here," Elizabeth whispered to Jeff.

"I didn't authorize anyone to touch his room," Mrs. Kottler said, her normal confidence shaken by this suspicious turn of events.

"Honestly. This must be some sick person's idea of a practical joke."

"Or a robbery," Hounslow said. "But why just his room?" He spun around to the three officers who had been waiting anxiously nearby, and pointed to the rookie who had originally called him on the radio. "You—search the grounds."

"Yes, sir," the officer squeaked and ran off.

"You two go room to room and talk to the residents and staff," Hounslow said to the other two. "Somebody has to know something. Those things didn't just walk out of here!"

"Be nice to my residents!" Mrs. Kottler called after the officers. "They're fragile!"

Hounslow glared at her. "Most of them are tough as nails. You don't have to worry."

Elizabeth thought about the moment she had escorted Dolly back to her room. She had just placed her hand on the doorknob to Adam's room when George Betterman stopped her. Had he been trying to keep her from seeing that the room was empty? She tried to recall the image in her mind. George Betterman in his wheelchair. The way he came down the hall toward her. There was something wrong with the way he looked. What was it?

Hounslow stepped into the room and surveyed the emptiness with his hands on his hips. He stood rigid and tense, his mouth set in a grim straight line.

"How long does it take to recharge a battery on a wheelchair?" Elizabeth suddenly whispered to Jeff.

Jeff looked at her, surprised. "I have no idea."

"Doug Hall was pushing George in his wheelchair at the Village. But when I saw him here just a few minutes later, it was running like always. Could he charge it that fast?"

"I doubt it."

Elizabeth was quiet for a moment. That was part of it, yes. But there was something else . . . something else.

"Bits," Jeff said, "maybe it's time you told the sheriff what you know."

73

"Let me get this straight," Hounslow said to Elizabeth in Mrs. Kottler's office. "One of the residents gives you the creeps because he thinks he knows you from somewhere else, you have a nightmare about him, then you get stuck in a closet and Mrs. Schultz has a heart attack because you *think* someone moved her pills."

Elizabeth frowned. She should have known he wouldn't listen. "She was *afraid* that night. She was acting really weird."

The sheriff leaned against Mrs. Kottler's desk and folded his arms. "Yeah, sure. And half the people in here will tell you she acted weird all the time. She was an eccentric."

Jeff, who'd been standing nearby quietly, moved forward. "What about George Betterman going into her room the next day?"

"What about it? He's a plant nut. He didn't want hers to go to waste, like he said. No offense, kids, but my father is missing, and I don't have time for your Sherlock Holmes routine." He stood up.

"Then how about George stopping me outside your father's room earlier?" Elizabeth challenged him.

Hounslow puffed out his cheeks peevishly. "If you had opened the door and seen whether the room was empty at that time, it would be helpful to me. Otherwise, all you have are your impressions of a man in a wheelchair who, by your own admission, 'bothers' you."

Elizabeth sat down with a sulky expression.

"What about the battery on the wheelchair?" Jeff asked, not ready to give up. "Why would Doug Hall be pushing him one minute at the Village, and the next minute Betterman's driving down the hallway?"

"Maybe he has a replacement battery. Maybe there were two different wheelchairs."

"He called me *Sarah*," Elizabeth snapped, bringing up the

one thing she knew better than to mention. "That was the name of the girl I switched places with in time."

Hounslow glared at her. "Don't start with Malcolm's time-travel mumbo-jumbo. I didn't believe it then, and I don't believe it now."

Jeff growled, "So you're not even going to question George Betterman?"

Hounslow frowned. "Oh, I'll question him, all right. But not because of what you've told me."

There was a knock at the door, then Mrs. Kottler peeked in nervously. "Sheriff? They're calling for you. It sounds important."

Hounslow bolted from the office as the rookie cop appeared breathlessly at the doorway to the reception area.

"What, Nick?" Hounslow asked.

Nick swallowed and choked, trying to catch his breath. "Outside . . . by the lake . . . quick!"

Hounslow pushed past him.

They sprinted out through the sliding glass doors in the recreation room, across the long stretch of lawn that reached toward the small manmade lake and the woods nearby. There was no doubt that they were all thinking the same thing: *Adam Hounslow has been found floating in the lake!*

But the two other police officers weren't at the lake. They stood thirty yards away at the edge of the woods and flagged their commander. The crowd followed Hounslow and his two men into the woods until they reached another officer who stood somberly by a large tree.

Elizabeth's heart pounded in sympathy with Hounslow as they approached.

"I found this cap," the officer said, holding up a red-and-yellow wool cap with a football team's logo stitched on the front. "Was this your dad's?"

Hounslow nodded quickly. "I got it for him for Christmas. They're his favorite team. You called me out here for a baseball cap?"

The officer pointed wordlessly to the ground. All eyes looked down.

"Oh no, " Hounslow whispered.

They were looking at a freshly filled-in hole, about the size of a grave.

It began to rain. Malcolm and Donald caught Manny Hurwitz, the owner of Miller's Antiques, just as he was locking up his shop. The original Miller had sold his business to Hurwitz three years before.

"What do you want?" Manny asked Malcolm and Donald when they walked up to the door. "See the sign? I'm closed."

"I'm Malcolm Dubbs and—"

Manny's eyes lit up. "Oh. Sorry, Mr. Dubbs, I didn't recognize you." He turned the key and pushed the door open. "Stay put. I have to turn off the burglar alarm." He disappeared inside for a moment, then returned and waved them in.

Manny glided through the room congested with antiques of all kinds. It reminded Malcolm of Donald's office. The biggest difference was that, where Donald was thin and angular, Manny was roly-poly with a doughboy face, round glasses, and thick, wiry hair.

"What can I do for you, Mr. Dubbs? Need a few more things for your Village? I'm here to serve."

"Actually, I need to find out about some items you already sold to us," Malcolm explained.

"I'll help if I can." He guided them back to his work area, a large oak desk surrounded by tall bookcases filled with reference books.

Donald pulled a computer printout from his jacket pocket. "We're trying to trace these three things. Normally we would have a detailed record, but these slipped through the cracks somehow."

Manny read the printout. "Hmm," he grunted, then turned to a large ledger next to his desk. He flipped open the long, lined pages and ran his finger up and down the columns.

"You're not on a computerized system?" Donald asked indignantly.

"Nope," Manny replied. "Fortunately, I remember these

three treasures. They were brought in just a couple of days ago. I won't have to look far."

Malcolm looked at Donald hopefully.

"Yep, there they are. Came in at the same time from the same person. Not valued very highly, I have to confess. But the seller insisted that I broker them to the Historical Village, no matter what the price. I promised I would."

"Who sold them to you?" Malcolm asked.

"According to my register, the owner was Adam Hounslow." Manny looked up from the book. "Any relation to Sheriff Hounslow?"

"Yes," Malcolm answered. "So Adam Hounslow sold the ring, shaving kit, and photo to you—but specifically for my Village."

Manny looked at Donald. "Isn't that what I just said?"

"Did he say anything else about it? Like, why he was selling them, or why he wanted them in the Village?"

Manny shook his head. "I didn't ask, and he didn't tell. Though I had to wonder why the sheriff's son would sell what were obviously family heirlooms. Is that what this is all about? The sheriff wants them back?"

"No. We're trying to establish—" Donald started to explain, but Malcolm cut him off.

"What did you say? The sheriff's *son*?"

"Well, yeah."

"But Adam Hounslow is Sheriff Hounslow's *father*."

Manny chuckled. "Young-looking father, then. The person who brought that stuff in was—oh, maybe twenty years old. Twenty-two tops."

"You'd better describe him for me," Malcolm said, yanking a pen from his pocket.

Manny handed him a piece of scrap paper from the desk. "That's easy," he said. "He was a good-looking kid. Deep dimples on both sides of his mouth. Curly brown hair, nice face, large brown eyes. Reminded me of a young Tony Curtis, you know? I kept thinking, this kid should be a movie star."

Because of the rain and the darkness, Hounslow brought out large tarps and powered lights. He cleared the area, forcing Jeff, Elizabeth, Mrs. Kottler, and other curious staff members to go back to the recreation room in the center. They crowded around the sliding glass door and watched from a distance. Nick, the rookie, had turned green when he saw the gravelike hole. Hounslow had told him to "wait at the center with the rest of the women and children." The sheriff remained, a bleak figure washed in the pouring rain watching the diggers.

The lights produced an eery glow in the woods that made the trees look like silhouettes of matchsticks.

"It's like a UFO has landed out there," Jeff observed.

The officers didn't have to dig for very long before Nick's radio came to life. "We found something . . . a box. A pretty big box, too."

Big enough to hold a shriveled old man? Nobody dared ask aloud the question all of them were thinking.

Nick looked green again. "What's in it?" he asked over his radio.

No one answered.

Malcolm arrived from Miller's Antiques just then, and looked to Jeff for a whispered explanation of what was happening.

The radio crackled.

"What?" Nick asked. "What is it?"

"It's . . . it's his stuff," the officer finally reported.

"Stuff?"

"The box is packed with the stuff from his room," the voice on the radio announced. "Looks like there's a second box with . . . yeah, more of the same. That's all."

Standing by the "gravesite," with the rain to hide his tears, Sheriff Richard Hounslow looked at the two boxes holding all that was left of his father's personal belongings. "Just what in blazes is going on here?" he shouted to no one in particular.

Hounslow stared at Malcolm from across the card table in the recreation room. His face was pale, his eyes void of their normal spark. "What did you find?"

"Your father's things were sold to the Village through Miller's Antiques—but your father didn't sell them. A young man did."

"Did this young man have a name?" Hounslow asked.

"No," Malcolm replied. "But Mr. Hurwitz, the owner, remembered what he looked like. Good-looking with deep dimples on both sides of his mouth. Curly brown hair and large brown eyes. Hurwitz said he reminded him of a young Tony Curtis. I guess he looked like a movie star."

Elizabeth and Mrs. Kottler both gasped, then looked at each other.

Hounslow looked up at them wearily. "Well? What's wrong?"

"You just described perfectly one of my employees," Mrs. Kottler said. "But I'm certain he wouldn't do anything illegal."

"What's his name?"

"Doug Hall."

"Where is he?"

"I believe he went to Hancock after he left the Village. He usually goes there for the weekend. Or sometimes Grantsville. I can't remember."

"Do you have an address or a contact number?"

"I might have one in the office records," she said.

The sheriff looked up at Deputy Peterson, who had joined them for the dig earlier. Peterson nodded.

"Come on, Mrs. Kottler. Let's have a look," he said and accompanied her out the door.

Hounslow flagged one of his other officers. "I want a complete rundown on this Hall kid. Talk to the residents, too."

"Mrs. Kottler isn't going to be very pleased with us for bothering the residents again," the officer said.

Hounslow slammed his palm against the tabletop. "I don't care!" he shouted, then visibly wrestled inside himself to calm down. "You're right. It won't help our situation if we kill the poor old dears from stress. We'll talk to them in the morning. Get everybody out except for the lab boys. I want fingerprints from my father's room and from those boxes in the hole. Rope the areas off."

"Yes, sir," the officer said and left.

"You must be tired," Hounslow said to Malcolm. "Busy day."

"A little," Malcolm agreed.

"Go home. All of you. There's nothing else for you to do here." He waved as if to shoo them away. "Go."

Jeff looked to his uncle for his assent. Malcolm nodded.

"Come on, Bits," Jeff whispered to Elizabeth, and they left.

Stepping into the hallway, Elizabeth saw something out of the corner of her eye. Down the corridor something or someone had moved. She didn't say anything to Jeff, but hesitated in her stride long enough to look quickly. A few doors away, she saw just the outline of the front of someone's legs and shoes peeking out. They silently withdrew into the doorway and disappeared from sight.

George Betterman.

"What's wrong?" Jeff asked.

"Nothing," she answered and caught up with him down the hall.

Her mind went back to that meeting with George Betterman outside of Adam Hounslow's room. Something was still bothering her . . . something her eyes picked up but her brain didn't register. Seeing the legs and shoes down the corridor just now put the image within reach, but she couldn't grab it.

Halfway home, Jeff finally broke her thoughtful silence. "Okay, tell me. What are you thinking about?"

"George Betterman."

"You can forget about him," Jeff snorted. "Hounslow won't be interested."

"Shoes," she muttered.

"What?"

"His shoes," she said louder, the picture forming in her mind. She had looked at his face, noted the trademark jogging suit and then his sneakers.

"What about his shoes?" Jeff asked.

Elizabeth turned in the passenger seat to face Jeff. "There was dirt and grass around the bottom of George's shoes."

Elizabeth groggily tugged at the belt on her robe and ambled into the kitchen. Alan and Jane Forde were at the table with half-filled cups of coffee and the remnants of grapefruit in front of them.

"Good morning, sleepyhead." Jane smiled.

"You're going to be late for church," Alan said from behind the Sunday paper.

Elizabeth focused on the front page of the paper, didn't see what she was looking for, then asked, "Is there anything about it?"

Alan spread the paper over top of everything on the table.

"Alan!" Jane protested and quickly retrieved her cup of coffee.

He pointed to a small article on the third page. "There."

Elizabeth moved around the table to look. SHERIFF'S FATHER MISSING, the headline said. The article stated that Adam Hounslow, elderly father of Sheriff Richard Hounslow, had gone missing while attending the opening of the Historical Village. Police were investigating.

"That's all?" she asked.

"Seems so." Alan took the paper. "You made the front page when you disappeared," he added casually.

Elizabeth shivered, and Jane shot a nasty look at her husband.

"Never mind." Elizabeth kissed her father on the top of his silver head as she walked past to get her breakfast. "It's okay, Mom," she said softly.

But the reminder of her own disappearance—and the reason for it—stayed with her through her meal, her quick shower, and the scramble to get to church.

To her parents' annoyance, they were a few minutes late and had to squeeze into the back row during the first hymn. Jeff, who sat several pews ahead, turned around to smile at her. Elizabeth wiggled her fingers at him and smiled back.

The service proceeded as usual until, right before his sermon, Reverend Armstrong suggested that the congregation pray for Adam Hounslow and the sheriff. "We've had our share of close calls and disappearances in this community," he said. "The anxiety this is causing our sheriff must be great. We should remember him in our hearts and our prayers until his father is returned safe and sound." And he led the church in a brief but eloquent prayer on behalf of the Hounslows.

Elizabeth wondered if the church had prayed for her when she disappeared. Maybe that helped to bring her back from the other time. Maybe it'll help bring Adam Hounslow back from wherever he was.

On the way out of church after the service, Elizabeth saw small clusters of her friends chatting amiably in the hall and on the steps. She waved but didn't join them. Instead she walked toward the small grove of trees along the east side of the church. Adam Hounslow's disappearance hadn't affected the beauty of the Sunday morning. Shafts of sunlight shot through the long branches. Elizabeth stepped into one, hoping its brightness might burn away the darkness hanging on the edge of her memories. Somehow whatever had happened to Adam Hounslow seemed linked to what had happened to her. She didn't know how or why, but she sensed it. The nightmare returned to her—the bath, the polluted water, the switch in time—and George Betterman sitting in her dark bedroom saying, "I know who you are . . . *Sarah.*"

"Excuse me."

Elizabeth jumped and spun around.

The speaker was a young woman Elizabeth had never seen before. "Sorry. I didn't mean to startle you. You're Elizabeth Forde, right?"

"Yes," Elizabeth said warily.

"I'm Jennifer Reeves. I was thinking about Adam Hounslow's disappearance, and I remembered that you were missing for a while too, weren't you?" She squinted as the shaft of light shifted and bleached her face.

Elizabeth was perplexed. "Who are you?"

"You disappeared under some very mysterious circumstances. I was wondering what you thought about Adam Hounslow's disappearance," the woman continued.

Elizabeth frowned. "You're a reporter, aren't you?"

"I just want to talk to you, that's all."

"Please leave me alone," Elizabeth said.

"Look, it'll help a lot of people if you'll just—"

"Get away from me!" Elizabeth shouted. It was enough to draw the attention of people still mingling outside the church. Jeff broke away from the small group he'd been talking to and raced toward her.

"What's wrong, Bits?"

Jennifer Reeves had turned and walked off, looking as if the whole scene bored her.

"She's a reporter," Elizabeth whispered.

Malcolm strode quickly across the lawn, followed by Alan and Jane Forde. Elizabeth felt foolish for the fuss she'd made.

"There's no problem," she said. "I'm sorry."

Jeff wouldn't let her get away with it. "That woman was a reporter," he announced.

"A reporter!" Malcolm exclaimed.

"I'll have a word or two with Jerry Anderson," Alan growled. Jerry was the editor of Fawlt Line's only daily newspaper.

"I don't think she works for him," Malcolm said as he watched the woman climb into a small rental car and drive off.

Jeff put his arm around Elizabeth. "Are you all right?" he asked anxiously.

She nodded. "Yeah. It's no big deal. She just annoyed me."

The five of them headed back toward the church and the parking lot beyond. Sheriff Hounslow was waiting for them next to his squad car.

"Good morning, Sheriff," Malcolm said.

"Any chance of talking to all of you?" Hounslow asked.

Malcolm glanced around at the others. "Why don't we go back to my cottage? Mrs. Packer makes a wonderful Sunday brunch."

Amidst the clinks and rattles of the cups and dishes on Malcolm's dining-room table, the small group made idle chitchat about the weather, the Village, anything other than the subject they were supposed to discuss. Alan Forde launched into a lengthy discussion about the air currents that were contributing to the weather patterns they were experiencing. His wife quietly asked him to shush. Finally, Mrs. Packer was complimented by all for a delicious lunch, and all eyes drifted to Sheriff Hounslow. He had called this meeting, so he needed to start it.

The sheriff wiped his mouth with a napkin and tossed it onto the table. "We haven't found Doug Hall yet," he announced. "We're still running a check on him."

"What happens next?" Alan asked.

"I don't know." Hounslow shook his head as he pushed away from the table. "What I have to say, I don't say easily. You know I'm not a big fan of all your time-travel mumbo jumbo. But I didn't sleep a wink last night, because I couldn't get it off my mind. I still think it's crazy, but I want to talk about it anyway. My father's still missing and—" He suddenly stopped, unable to go on. He turned away from them until he could compose himself.

"Your father's missing and, like any good detective, you want to consider all the possibilities," Malcolm said, giving him time to recover.

The sheriff cleared his throat. "Something like that. So you talk, and I'll listen."

Malcolm stood up and paced around the table as he spoke. "It's taken me a long time to figure it out, but I believe that Fawlt Line is located not on a geographical fault, but a *time* fault. That's why Elizabeth disappeared and how King Arthur slipped through. It's possible that your father stumbled onto another fault—a doorway, if you will—in the miners' row houses."

"Stumbled? Like tripping on a rock and suddenly falling to some other time? An accident?"

"Maybe." Malcolm gave his ear a habitual tug. "Though I'm not a big believer in accidents or coincidences. I'm inclined toward a more providential point of view."

"I don't think this is an accident, either," Hounslow said. "Whatever happened to my father happened on purpose."

"What makes you so sure?" Jeff asked.

The question was harmless enough, but it touched a deep place in the sheriff. He struggled for a moment, then finally said, "I'm sorry. My father is all I have left and, well, we haven't been getting along lately. I had to practically carry him out of the house he'd lived in for years. It was too big for him to take care of. And my dad was showing the early signs of Alzheimer's disease."

"Difficult. Very difficult," Alan said softly.

"He had reached a point of despair in his life like I've never seen before—not even when my mother died." Hounslow gestured to Elizabeth. "You saw how grouchy he was at the center. Well, that wasn't my dad. He was always a good-humored man. But twice in the last several months—when he was still living in his house—I went to see him and actually thought he was dead. He was just lying there with virtually no vital signs. I called the ambulance and everything."

"What was wrong with him?" Elizabeth asked.

"The doctors didn't have an explanation, except that it might've been psychological. They thought he was overwhelmed with the desire to die." The sheriff fiddled with the tablecloth. "Going to the retirement center was probably the icing on the cake. That's what I mean when I say it wasn't an accident. I think my father ran away somehow or, more likely . . . killed himself."

The room was stiff with silence. Hounslow caught a sob in his throat, and Jeff and Elizabeth looked at each other uneasily. They weren't sure how to react to their realization that beyond the sheriff's loud bark, he was very human. Alan and Jane stared at the table. They were remembering their own feelings when Elizabeth had disappeared.

Malcolm slipped next to the sheriff and put a comforting hand on his shoulder. "You don't really believe that, do you?"

"Oh, yes," Hounslow replied. "I've thought and rethought my father's behavior yesterday. There was a certain peace, a strange calm, as if he knew this was going to happen. He *knew*."

The sheriff lowered his head and said nothing else. Malcolm looked to Jeff, Elizabeth, Alan, and Jane as if to say that now was the right time for them to leave. They nodded and quietly stood up and walked out of the dining room.

"You'll bring Elizabeth home?" Alan asked Jeff.

"Yes, sir."

"Keep the reporters away from her," Jane admonished him.

"Yes, ma'am."

Alan and Jane made their way to the front door and out to their car beyond. Elizabeth and Jeff slipped through Malcolm's den, then outside through the glass doors, and sat on the patio.

"I should tell him about the dirt and grass on the bottoms of George Betterman's shoes," Elizabeth said, stretching like a cat in the hot sun.

"He wouldn't believe you," Jeff said.

Elizabeth looked doubtful. "I think he would. He looks ready to believe anything that'll help him find his dad."

Jeff frowned. "Even if he did cry a little, he's still the same stubborn man. Do you think he'll believe that a man in a wheel-chair suddenly leapt up to kidnap his father?"

"But we don't know that George really needs to be in a wheelchair. What if he's been faking it all along?"

Jeff thought about it for a moment. "Mrs. Kottler might know. Or the records at the retirement center probably say why he's in the chair."

They looked at each other, then Jeff smiled. "What do you say we take a little Sunday drive over to the retirement center and find out for ourselves?"

In the dining room, Hounslow stood up. "It's more than I can believe."

Malcolm smiled. "Who could believe it? If it hadn't happened to Elizabeth—if she hadn't experienced that other time firsthand—I'd be skeptical, too. But she did experience it. So did Jeff. We saw their time-twins for ourselves."

"King Arthur didn't have a time-twin," Hounslow argued.

"That was different," Malcolm said. "And I can't explain why any more than I can explain how your father might have disappeared in the row house. But he might have. By accident or on purpose. Only he knows right now."

"And you really think he's alive?"

For the first time since their conversation began, Malcolm looked troubled. "I wish I could say so for sure. I can't."

Hounslow nodded sadly. "Well, I have to go back to the station. We've got an all-points bulletin out on Doug Hall. Right now he's the only solid lead we have."

CHAPTER 17

The retirement center was thick with the lethargy of the Sunday heat. At least, that's what Jeff and Elizabeth decided. As they searched for Mrs. Kottler, they couldn't seem to get more than a quick "hello" from the residents they saw in the halls or sitting in the recreation room.

"Are they always so pleasant?" Jeff asked sarcastically.

"Something's wrong," Elizabeth whispered back. "Maybe they're still upset about the death of Mrs. Schultz and the disappearance of Mr. Hounslow."

"Maybe."

They found Dolly Higgins sitting alone in her room. She looked up apprehensively when Elizabeth knocked on her door and entered.

"Hi, Dolly!" Elizabeth said cheerfully.

"What are you doing here, child? It's Sunday."

"I'm allowed to come visit you if I want to, aren't I?" Elizabeth smiled.

Dolly frowned. "If you want, I suppose. But . . . I'm feeling tired. I really shouldn't have visitors right now."

"Well, it's a perfect afternoon for a nap," Elizabeth replied sympathetically and scooted Jeff out of the room.

"This is weird," she said when they were out of earshot. "And Mrs. Kottler isn't anywhere around. Let's go look for the files."

Elizabeth led Jeff through the front reception area to Mrs. Kottler's office. Her door was locked, and Elizabeth felt relieved. Sneaking around in the filing cabinets suddenly struck her as a bad idea.

"What about this one?" Jeff asked, moving to a door on the opposite wall.

Elizabeth didn't remember where it led. "It might be a closet."

Jeff jiggled the handle, and the door opened easily. He peeked in. "It looks like a little kitchen." He disappeared into the room, so that Elizabeth could only hear his voice. "Hey, there's another door."

Elizabeth glanced around to make sure no one could see them, then followed him in. "I don't think we should do this," she said.

But Jeff had gone through a door at the other end of the kitchen area—into Mrs. Kottler's office. He was already at one of the filing cabinets, rifling through the manila folders. "Betterman . . . Betterman . . ." he muttered.

"I don't like this, Jeff," Elizabeth said. "It's probably against the law."

"We're not stealing anything. A quick peek at George's file is all we want."

"Well, hurry," she said. She heard something in the other room and tiptoed through the kitchen. She peered out the door into the reception area. Still empty. But then an unmistakable sound from down the hall sent a hard chill through her body. It was the whirring of an electric motor.

Then she heard Mrs. Kottler's voice. "Now, Mr. Betterman, I know what you're thinking. . . ."

Elizabeth gently closed the door and raced back into Mrs. Kottler's office. "Jeff!" she whispered.

"Found it!" he said.

"Put it away! They're coming!" she cried.

Jeff looked stricken and fumbled as he tried to shove the file back into the drawer.

The whir and the voice were closer, probably in the reception area. Jeff dropped the file. It fell to the floor and sent pages, like shocked birds, into several directions.

Elizabeth's mind seized up. All she could think to do was create a diversion somehow by running through the little kitchen and into the reception area. Then Mrs. Kottler's key turned in the lock.

It must've been quite a picture for Mrs. Kottler and George Betterman when they entered the room. Elizabeth stood at the kitchen door with her hand clasped over her mouth. Jeff crouched over the scattered pages.

"Good heavens!" Mrs. Kottler cried.

"What's going on here?" George growled.

Jeff stood up, but didn't speak. George drove his wheelchair forward and snatched up a page from the floor.

"Elizabeth!" Mrs. Kottler exclaimed when she noticed her near the kitchen. "What's the meaning of this?"

"This is *my* file," George said. "What are you up to? Why are you looking at my file?"

Lost for a reasonable excuse, Jeff blurted out the truth. "Because we think you have something to do with Adam Hounslow's disappearance."

"What?" Mrs. Kottler shrieked.

Elizabeth moved to Jeff's side. "Mrs. Kottler, there's a lot going on here that you—"

"Do you know I could have you arrested for this? How dare you break into my office and steal one of my resident's files?"

George waved at Mrs. Kottler to be quiet. "What are you talking about? What makes you think I have anything to do with Adam Hounslow?"

"The dirt and grass on your shoes after Mr. Hounslow disappeared, for one thing," Elizabeth said as a challenge. "I saw it when you stopped me from going into his room. Your shoes were filthy, like you'd been out in the woods where they found Mr. Hounslow's stuff."

George clucked his tongue and shook his head at her. "Girl, you have too much time on your hands. I'll tell you what happened—"

"No, Mr. Betterman," Mrs. Kottler said coldly. "Don't satisfy their warped curiosity."

Betterman went on anyway. "I hit a pothole in the lawn, and it sent me and my wheelchair tumbling. My feet skidded along the dirt and grass. It was very painful for me."

Jeff and Elizabeth were both at a loss for words. But Jeff wasn't ready to give up. "So why do you keep calling Elizabeth *Sarah*, huh? Why are you trying to scare her?"

"This is ridiculous," George snarled and abruptly spun his wheelchair around to leave. "I leave them in your charge, Mrs. Kottler."

Mrs. Kottler glared at them. "I don't care if you are the nephew of Malcolm Dubbs or the Prince of Wales. I want you out of here . . . now."

"Mrs. Kottler, listen," Elizabeth said quickly. "You don't know what's going on. Something's happening here, and Mr. Betterman's in the middle of it."

"I'm so disappointed in you, Elizabeth," Mrs. Kottler said. "Your volunteer services are no longer wanted here. I should call the police, but I won't. Just go."

"Mrs. Schultz's death . . . Adam Hounslow's disappearance . . . *please*, Mrs. Kottler! Check into George Betterman! That's the only reason we did this. We wanted to see if he really should be in a wheelchair."

Mrs. Kottler pointed to the door. "Go."

Jeff moved past her and pulled at Elizabeth's arm. "Let's go, Bits. It's no use."

"You're in on it too, aren't you?" Elizabeth suddenly accused her.

Mrs. Kottler gasped indignantly.

"You're part of it somehow. That's the only way it could go on. You're in cahoots with George Betterman."

"Get out now, or I'll have the police here so fast your head will swim!" the director shouted.

Elizabeth turned silently away. Whatever was going on with George Betterman, the retirement center, and Adam Hounslow wouldn't be uncovered by her—not like this. But she knew as she walked out of the office that she wouldn't be free of her nightmares until the truth was known.

CHAPTER 18

Deputy Bob Peterson, with dark circles of sweat around the arms of his uniform, dropped another collection of faxes onto the table in the police station's conference room. "A few more answers from the nursing homes," he announced.

Hounslow looked up. "Anything from Hancock or from Grantsville?"

"No," Peterson said. "Doug Hall seems to have dropped off the face of the earth."

"Maybe *he* slipped through your time fault," Hounslow jabbed at Malcolm, who was flipping through faxes at the end of the table.

"Jeff and Elizabeth saw him pushing George Betterman's wheelchair out of the Village, remember?" Malcolm countered.

"Which is the only reason I'm still hoping that my dad is with Hall somewhere."

Malcolm leaned back in his chair. He hadn't thought of that possibility. "What did Betterman say when you asked him about Doug Hall? Obviously he was one of the last to see him."

" 'He's a nice boy' was about all George had to offer. He said Doug dropped him off at the center and then took off for a 'wild weekend away,' " the sheriff grumbled. "What kind of wild weekend can anyone have in Hancock or Grantsville?"

"What did the rest of the residents say about him?"

"The women at the center loved him. Apparently he was a real charmer."

Malcolm sighed, then gestured to the papers. "Why would such a charming young man switch jobs so often? And all in nursing homes. Two a year in the past six years."

"Sheriff," Peterson interrupted. "I checked on missing persons reports in all the towns where Doug Hall worked before now."

Hounslow grunted appreciatively. "Good thinking, Bob."

"I don't know what to make of it, but—" he held up a couple of the pages "—it looks like there have been a couple of cases of people disappearing from areas where Doug Hall worked."

"*What?!?*" Hounslow roared.

Jeff drove Elizabeth home. A broody silence had settled over them in the car. Apart from the humiliation they'd just suffered with Mrs. Kottler and George Betterman, they felt the agony of helplessness. To know that something bad—perhaps even *evil*, as Frieda Schultz had said—was going on and not be able to do anything about it was more than either of them could stand. Elizabeth was surprised to realize that she'd moved from a fear of George Betterman to a defiant anger at him.

Her parents were in the middle of their usual Sunday afternoon activities when she and Jeff arrived. Her father was pulling weeds in the garden, her mother ironing some clothes in the laundry room.

"I'm going to get out of my church dress and into some jeans," Elizabeth told Jeff.

"Wait a minute," Jane Forde called out. "Take these clothes up with you."

Elizabeth walked into the laundry room to grab her freshly pressed shirts and pants from the rack. "Thanks, Mom." She noticed that her uniform from the retirement center was included in the collection. "Oh. I forgot about this," she said.

"It was filthy," Mrs. Forde declared. "And you left some things in the pockets. I almost washed them."

"Sorry," Elizabeth said and retrieved a couple of tissues and a scrap of paper. "Thanks for cleaning it."

"Well, you can't go to the center tomorrow with a dirty uniform."

Elizabeth looked at her mother, then Jeff, who was leaning against the door post. "I'm not going back to the center."

"You're not?"

Elizabeth sighed. "You tell her while I change," she said to Jeff.

"Thanks a lot," he answered.

Elizabeth took her clothes up to her room, hung them in her closet, and quickly changed into a T-shirt and jeans. She was tying the shoelaces on her sneakers when her eye caught the scrap of paper her mom had pulled from her uniform pocket.

"Gloxinia" an elderly scrawl stated simply at the top. Elizabeth felt a tug at her heart. It was Frieda Schultz's handwriting. She'd written down the name of her flowers for Elizabeth the very day she'd died. Elizabeth gently took the scrap and unfolded it. *Poor Frieda,* she thought. *Will anyone ever know what really happened to you? Why did you cry so mournfully?*

Elizabeth's eyes widened. Beneath the name of the flowers, Mrs. Schultz had scribbled, "*Help. Fawlt Line Cinema. 10:00 p.m. 22nd.*"

She stared at the piece of paper for a moment, trying to register what it might mean. Why had Mrs. Schultz written such a cryptic message?

Because she was scared, Elizabeth realized. She was trying to communicate with Elizabeth while she had the chance. But what did it mean?

Shoving the scrap into her pocket, she made her way downstairs and found Jeff in the den with Jane Forde. Alan had joined them, grimy and sweaty from the garden. When she walked in, her parents looked at her with worried expressions.

"You never should have gone into that office," Alan Forde reprimanded her. "It's against the law and, if your suspicions are true, potentially dangerous."

Elizabeth hung her head. "I know. But we never could've gotten the police in there. It seemed like a good idea at the time."

"You're both lucky Mrs. Kottler didn't have you locked up," Mrs. Forde said.

Jeff fidgeted in his chair. "I wish she would've called the police. Chances are it would've forced them to check into what we've been saying."

Alan chuckled. "All you have are suspicions, guesses, and

feelings. The police have no way of forcing George Betterman to admit to anything. And it's entirely possible that you're wrong."

"What?" Elizabeth asked, stunned.

"If you want to play detective, then play well," Alan said. "A good detective considers all possibilities, I heard your Uncle Malcolm say today."

Elizabeth pulled the scrap from her pocket. "If I'm wrong, then what about this?" She passed the note around. "It's a message from Frieda Schultz—right before she died. She said she was writing down the name of her flowers. I forgot all about it till Mom found it today. "

Alan pondered the note for a moment. "Maybe she wrote the name of the flowers over top a note she'd written to herself."

Elizabeth glared at him. "Oh, Daddy, you're as bad as Sheriff Hounslow! Why would she write 'help' on a note to herself?"

"Maybe the cinema needs it," he offered.

Mrs. Forde rubbed her chin. "But Fawlt Line doesn't have a cinema anymore."

"It doesn't?" Alan asked.

"It closed down a few years ago, remember?" she replied.

"Then Uncle Malcolm moved it to the Village," Jeff added.

"Yes, yes!" Alan interjected, the light coming on in his eyes. "He said it was a perfect example of a 1930s movie theater, with its balconies and gold trimmings and the big old burgundy curtain."

"I think we should take the note to the police," Jeff suggested.

"Sensible thinking, Jeff," Alan commended him.

In Jeff's Volkswagen once again, they chugged along to the station. Jeff glanced knowingly over at Elizabeth. "You know what today is," he said.

"Sunday?"

"The twenty-second. Mrs. Schultz's note said ten o'clock tonight."

The police department was a beehive of unusual activity. Jeff and Elizabeth made their way past the harried-looking men and women who were shouting into phones or darting back and forth between the small offices. The center of the activity was a conference room at the end of the hall, where Hounslow was barking orders at whoever happened to be handy.

"I don't care if it's late on a Sunday afternoon or midnight on Christmas Eve! Tell them this is an emergency!" the sheriff shouted at one frazzled woman.

Jeff and Elizabeth quietly walked in, spotted Malcolm, and joined him at his end of the table.

"What's going on, Uncle Malcolm?"

"They're calling police departments around the country," Malcolm explained. "We found a connection between Doug Hall's employment and other unsolved missing-persons cases."

Elizabeth gasped. "You think Doug Hall kidnapped Adam Hounslow?"

"We don't know anything at this point. Because it's Sunday, we've had a hard time tracking down the investigating officers, or even someone who might be able to pull a file. All we need are some details about the missing people." Malcolm rubbed his face wearily. "I'm afraid this could take all night. There must be a way to talk to at least one of the investigators face-to-face."

"Look at this!" Hounslow cried to no one in particular. He was pointing at the accumulated bits of information in front of him on the table. "Why didn't we see this? If it were a snake it would've bit me." He turned to Malcolm. "Look. In most of these cases, maybe all of them, the missing person disappeared in—well, here. Look for yourself!"

Malcolm flipped through some pages. "This one disappeared in a historic bed-and-breakfast in Boston—"

"Three blocks from the nursing home where Hall worked," Hounslow added.

"This one disappeared in a Baltimore museum," Malcolm continued. "A historic mansion, another museum, a library, the oldest building in a college . . . a restaurant?"

"It was closed," Hounslow explained.

"So they all disappeared in historical places," Jeff said.

"Coincidence?" Deputy Peterson asked.

"What do *you* think?" Hounslow challenged him. "You've got Doug Hall and people disappearing in places of historical interest. Just like my dad. How did the investigating officers miss this? Why wasn't Hall ever arrested?"

"Who could've made a connection until now?" Malcolm asked, in defense of all the investigators who weren't there to answer for themselves.

Hounslow waved his arms at his staff. "Don't just stand around! Get back on the phones! I want this confirmed! I want to know about the rest of these cases!"

Everyone scattered, except Malcolm, Jeff, and Elizabeth. Hounslow slumped into his chair and put his face in his hands.

There was a pause long enough to give Elizabeth the courage to step forward, the scrap of paper from Mrs. Schultz in her outstretched hand. "Sheriff? We thought you might want to see this."

He lifted his head up slightly and took the scrap. "What is it?"

"Mrs. Schultz wrote it before she died." Elizabeth rounded the table and guided him through the message. "Gloxinia is the name of the flower she had on her night stand—the plant George Betterman took away."

"Oh, please. You're not going to start on this whole Betterman business again," Hounslow complained.

"No, sir," Elizabeth continued. "But look at the rest of the note . . . 'Help!' Then the cinema at ten o'clock tonight."

"Meaning?"

"Meaning that maybe something will happen there tonight," she said, puzzled that he hadn't figured it out for himself.

Hounslow groaned, then tossed the note onto the table. "All right. If I have someone available, I'll try to remember to send him over."

"The cinema's at the Village," Malcolm said. "I can have one of my security guards check in on it."

"Whatever," Hounslow said dismissively, then spread his arms over the pages and pages of reports. "This is going to take too long. And probably none of it has anything to do with my father's disappearance." He suddenly pounded the tabletop. "Blast it, Hall! Where are you?"

Malcolm leaned forward and thoughtfully picked up a small, clipped stack of papers. He looked at them for a moment, then turned to Hounslow. "Sheriff, this case happened only a year ago in Annapolis. Doug Hall worked at a nursing home on West Street, and a man disappeared in the Colonial Book Shop nearby. If I flew down in my plane, I'd be there within an hour."

"I can't ask you to do that," Hounslow said.

"You don't have to, I'm suggesting it myself. I could talk to the detective who handled the case, providing you can use your authority to have him or her meet me. It's worth a try, right?"

Hounslow looked as if he might argue, then changed his mind. "All right. If you don't have anything better to do." Which was Hounslow's way of saying he was grateful.

"Do you want to come with me, Jeff? It'd be helpful to have a partner."

"Are you kidding?" Jeff beamed. "You couldn't keep me away!"

Elizabeth cleared her throat loudly.

"I'm sorry, Elizabeth," Malcolm said. "I think three will make things a little complicated and crowded. We don't want to look like we're ganging up on the poor detective."

"That's okay," she replied, then gestured for Jeff to come talk to her privately. They retreated to a corner.

"What's wrong?" Jeff whispered.

"What about the cinema at ten o'clock?"

"Uncle Malcolm will have one of his guards check it out."

"And what am I supposed to do in the meantime?" Elizabeth was annoyed.

"We won't be gone that long, Bits. We'll be home in no time at all."

"Mind if I wait for you at Uncle Malcolm's?" Elizabeth asked as a concession. "I don't want to be far away if you come back with any news."

"Suits me," Jeff said.

Jeff drove Elizabeth to the cottage in his Volkswagen, and Malcolm arrived a minute later in his jeep. Mrs. Packer had been watching for them, and ran out to the driveway to greet them.

"What's wrong?" Malcolm called, without getting out of the car.

"Mr. Nelson keeps calling for you. He says he needs to talk to you right away."

"Probably some business to do with the Village," Malcolm mumbled to himself. To Mrs. Packer he said, "Tell him I'll be back later tonight, probably around nine-thirty. I'll call him then."

Mrs. Packer frowned. "He won't like it."

"He'll get over it," Malcolm said. "Oh—and will you please call the security office and ask them to check the Old Cinema at ten o'clock?"

"Yes, sir," she said, then looked up in surprise. "At ten o'clock?"

Malcolm smiled and wound up his window. "Let's go, Jeff," he called out.

Jeff had gotten into the passenger seat and was talking to Elizabeth through the window. He kissed her lightly on the lips and gently stroked her hair. "We'll be back in no time at all, Bits."

She nodded and stepped away from the car.

Malcolm reversed out of the driveway, and Mrs. Packer and Elizabeth stood side by side waving as the jeep pulled away.

CHAPTER 19

Annapolis was the first capital of the American colonies and still maintained much of its colonial appearance in the historic district surrounding the State House. The Naval Academy, Chesapeake Bay, Severn River and harbor were all within a mile of the red-and-black brick police headquarters nestled in a small wood off Taylor Avenue. Somehow it seemed so civilized, Jeff thought.

Detective Steve White had been caught by Sheriff Hounslow just as he returned from his traditional Sunday spent crabbing on the river. Even though he'd showered and changed clothes, he still smelled of seawater and fish when he shook Malcolm's and Jeff's hands. His face was beet red and looked nearly comical sitting atop broad shoulders on a short, stocky body.

"I don't think I put enough suntan lotion on," he explained as he gestured to the wooden visitor chairs opposite his desk.

Malcolm and Jeff sat down.

"Thank you for seeing us on your day off," Malcolm said. "We appreciate your help."

Detective White tilted his head slightly. "Pretty odd circumstances, I'd say. Particularly your sheriff sending two civilians to look at our files. I had to clear it with my commander." He slid two manila folders across the desk toward Malcolm. "These are copies of what we have. You can take them back to Hounslow. Did I understand that it's his father who disappeared?"

Malcolm nodded and picked up the file. "Uh-huh. It's quite a mystery."

"Then let's compare some notes," White suggested. "I was the detective on the two cases of missing persons we had here at the time. The first was Ralph McInery. He was living at the Arundel Nursing Home where Doug Hall worked. McInery's the one who went into the Colonial Book Shop on West Street and, as far as anyone knows, never came out again."

"How was that possible? Somebody must have noticed."

"It happened at the height of the tourist season last summer. People were in and out of the shop constantly. The employees simply didn't remember what happened after he came in. The whole business was reported by Jack Greene, a friend of McInery's from the home. They were shopping together. Greene said McInery went into the store but didn't come out again."

"Back door?"

"Yes. But the manager of the store was there the whole time doing inventory. Nobody came through." White pointed to the second file. "That case involved a guy named Thomas Finney. He also lived at the Arundel Nursing Home and disappeared from an antique shop in one of those old houses near the harbor. It was during the tourist season, too, toward the end of the summer. He went in with a group of senior citizens, but didn't come out again. We nearly tore the house apart looking for him."

"I guess the big question is: why wasn't Doug Hall brought in?" Malcolm asked.

White grimaced. "On what charges? It's not like we had any evidence of foul play. All we could do was establish that Hall knew the missing people and was in the area when they disappeared."

"What do you mean, 'in the area'?"

"He was in the Colonial Book Shop the day McInery disappeared—ditto the antique shop when Finney went bye-bye. But that wasn't unusual. Hall was responsible for transporting the residents when they went shopping. I couldn't arrest him for doing his job."

"Of course not," Malcolm said as he thumbed through the file.

"Don't get me wrong," White went on. "I suspected Hall when I realized he'd been an employee in other towns where old folks disappeared. And, frankly, I didn't like him. He was too smooth, if you know what I mean. So we kept an eye on him. But it didn't lead anywhere, and when Hall decided to leave town, we had no grounds to stop him."

"Did you ever find the missing people?" Jeff asked.

"Nope. Both cases are unsolved. Without a kidnapper's note or discovery of a body, the feeling was that the two men had run away of their own free will."

Malcolm raised an eyebrow. "Why did you think that?"

"Because of their states of mind before they disappeared. We learned from folks they knew at the home that both men were extremely unhappy there. But before they disappeared they seemed to have a certain . . . peace . . . like suicides sometimes have before they do the deed."

"Hmm," said Malcolm. "That's how Sheriff Hounslow described his father before he disappeared."

"That's interesting. Does he think his father committed suicide?"

Malcolm shrugged. "I don't think he's ruling anything out at this point."

"It's gotta be awful for him—investigating his own father's disappearance. He said it happened at that historical village? I saw something about it in the newspapers. Maybe I'll make a weekend of it and come up with my family sometime."

"Please do," Malcolm said. "Give me enough warning and I'll make sure you get in free."

"Thanks." The detective looked genuinely pleased.

"Did any of your investigators make the connection that these two missing men both disappeared in places of historical interest?"

"Not really. Hey, all of the buildings in this part of town are historical. We would've written it off as coincidence. But there was one small curious bit of information that came up. I didn't think much of it at the time. Even if I had, I'm not sure I would've figured out what it meant."

Malcolm and Jeff waited while White searched through the files.

"Here," he finally said. "The missing men had previously

done business with the places where they disappeared."

Malcolm sat up. "What?"

White seemed pleased to get Malcolm's attention so dramatically. "McInery had sold his entire library—a lot of books, I guess—to the Colonial Book Shop two weeks before he disappeared. And Finney sold several boxes of family heirlooms to the antique shop. Does that mean something to you?"

"Adam Hounslow sold some of his belongings to my Village. But he did it through Doug Hall and a local antique shop!"

A question suddenly occurred to Jeff, and he automatically raised his hand. Then, realizing that he wasn't in school, he quickly pulled it back down. "How did the people at the nursing home respond when McInery and Finney disappeared?"

White rubbed his chin for a moment, then spoke slowly as he tried to remember. "If I remember correctly, they were agitated and alarmed. Pretty much as you'd expect people to be after their friends go missing. Some were very suspicious, I think. And, you know, now that you mention it, they seemed to close up on me. Nobody wanted to talk or answer questions. As if they were scared. But I figured that was normal, all things considered. Why?"

"Because that's how everybody was acting at the Fawlt Line Retirement Center today," Jeff replied. Malcolm looked at Jeff with interest.

"Pretty normal, I'd guess," White concluded. "Those nursing homes can be tightly wound communities. The people who live there sometimes circle the wagons to ward off any outside threat." He paused, then put his hands on his desk and stood up. "Well, look, if you two will excuse me, I have a family at home who need me to get the meat out of the crabs I caught today."

Malcolm and Jeff walked out with Detective White, and Malcolm thanked him again for taking the time to talk to them.

White shook their hands again. "Don't hesitate to call me tomorrow, if you need any more information. I hope Sheriff Hounslow finds his father."

Malcolm and Jeff got into their rental car and drove back to the small airfield on the outskirts of town.

"Too many coincidences," Jeff said.

Malcolm agreed. "These aren't coincidences. They're patterns of some kind. But what do they mean? What in the world is Doug Hall up to?"

CHAPTER 20

The summer light had moved across the wall and was fading into night when Sheriff Hounslow poured himself his seventh cup of coffee. He set it on the littered table and stretched with a loud groan. The thought of yet another round with the reports didn't appeal to him at all. He wanted to get out and *do* something to find his father. But there wasn't much to do, except go through the reports and hope to find a link, a piece of information, *anything* that might give him a lead to his father's whereabouts. He sat down and wearily picked up the cup to take a sip of the bitter-tasting liquid.

"Sheriff!" Deputy Peterson shouted, causing Hounslow to dribble hot coffee on his chin.

"Doggone it, Bob!" Hounslow exclaimed as he grabbed a napkin and tried to keep the coffee off his shirt.

"Oh, sorry," Peterson stammered. "I just thought you'd want to know that Doug Hall's car was seen at a boarding house outside of Grantsville."

"Did you get the address?"

"Yeah."

That was all the sheriff needed to hear. "Let's go!" he barked, grabbing his hat and heading for the door.

"But that's outside our jurisdiction! The Grantsville Police will—"

Hounslow brushed past him. "The Grantsville Police will appreciate our help. I'm going."

Deputy Peterson shrugged helplessly and chased his boss down the hall.

Elizabeth and Mrs. Packer were in Malcolm's study playing checkers when the phone on the desk rang. The housekeeper reached over to get it.

"Dubbs's Cottage . . . Where are you, Mr. Dubbs?"

At the mention of Malcolm's name, Elizabeth perked up. "Are they back? Did they find out anything?"

Mrs. Packer signaled her to be quiet. "Oh, that's too bad."

"What?" Elizabeth asked.

"They're going to be late," Mrs. Packer told her, covering the mouthpiece. "They're grounded in Annapolis due to cloud cover." She turned her attention back to Malcolm. "Elizabeth is champing at the bit to know what you've learned . . . Yes. Oh, and Don Nelson has been calling for you. Do you have his number? . . . Yes. Thank you. We'll be here."

"Well?" Elizabeth asked anxiously.

"He said they've learned plenty, and he'll tell you all about it in a few hours—if your parents will let you stay here and wait."

Elizabeth looked at her apprehensively. "Do you mind?"

"Not at all."

"Then I'll call them."

"Sorry it took so long to get back to you, Donald," Malcolm apologized over a crackly telephone line.

"Quite all right." Donald Nelson cradled the phone between his cheek and shoulder as he tugged at a list he'd placed on the edge of his desk.

"What's so important?"

Donald cleared his throat. "Well, because of the situation with Adam Hounslow's belongings, I thought I'd double-check any other local purchases we've made for the Village."

"Smart thinking."

"I've been going through the inventory records, cross-referencing what we've purchased from all the local antique shops, and discovered a rather bizarre connection."

The line hissed for a moment. "We're full of bizarre connections tonight," Malcolm said. "What did you find?"

"For the most part," Donald began, "the antiques we bought for the Village were from a wide variety of sources. A hurricane lamp from the Andrews family, a turn-of-the-century sewing machine from the Smiths, china from the Stevensons. Unless we hit on a family auction or bankruptcy, our antique purchases are generally quite diversified."

"We get a lot of different things from a lot of different places," Malcolm said simply. "Is that what you're saying?"

"Yes, sir."

"And?"

"Well, as I've been tracing our local purchases, I've discovered that the majority of the antiques were supplied by a minority of families, fewer than a dozen in all."

"In other words," said Malcolm, "we got a lot of different things from only a few places. I'm with you so far. Is that it?"

"No, sir," Donald replied. "I contacted the antique shops—no small feat on a Sunday, by the way—and they led me to the names of the people who sold the antiques to them in the first place. I then began calling those names to talk to whoever made the sale. I didn't get through to them all, but those I actually contacted had no idea what I was talking about."

"What do you mean?"

"They were families who had no idea that their heirlooms had been donated or sold. When I asked who had the authority to sell the items, in almost every case it was, say, an elderly mother or father."

"Like Adam Hounslow, for example."

"Naturally, I asked the families how I might get in touch with their elderly parents, and they all said I could visit them at the nursing home where they lived. . . . Three guesses which nursing home."

The line hissed and sputtered again. "Tell me exactly what you're thinking, Donald."

"Well, I have to wonder if Doug Hall 'fenced' those antiques for everyone else the way he did for Adam Hounslow—with or without their permission. I don't suppose we'll know until he's caught. But I felt certain you would want to know."

"And you were right, Donald. I only wish I had called you

sooner." The line was silent for another moment, then Malcolm spoke again. "And Donald? There's something else I need you to do right away."

CHAPTER 21

By the time Sheriff Hounslow and Deputy Peterson reached the small boarding house where Doug Hall's car had been seen, the Grantsville police, under the command of Captain Louis Bly, had already invaded it. Doug Hall's car wasn't there. Neither was Doug Hall.

Hounslow flashed his badge and pushed past the Grantsville officers who were trying to calm the bewildered landlady in the front hall. Other patrolmen were interviewing tenants in the doorways to their rooms. Louis Bly was at the top of the stairs and signaled for Hounslow to follow him.

"Sorry we couldn't wait for you. The call went out on the monitor, and I was afraid he might hear it and run. He was gone by the time we got here anyway." They entered Doug Hall's room, a sparsely decorated apartment with the most basic necessities: a bed, a dresser, and a sink.

"Looks like he plans to come back," Hounslow said, referring to the overnight case that sat open in the corner.

"We'll be here if he does," Bly confirmed.

Hounslow knelt next to the case. "Anything in here except clothes?"

"A toothbrush," Bly answered. "Oh, and those receipts. I was about to look through them when they said you'd arrived."

Hounslow picked up the small bundle of papers, wrapped with a rubber band, and flipped through them. "These are receipts, all right. From antique shops in the area."

"Hall buys antiques?"

"Apparently he's been *selling* them." The bill of sale for his father's shaving kit, ring, and photo was included. The rest of them had familiar names written on them—all names of people Hounslow had talked to at the retirement center.

"Selling them legitimately, or is he a fence for stolen antiques?"

Hounslow suddenly realized that he didn't know. What if his father had given Hall permission to sell those family treasures? What if *all* the people at the center had? To Hounslow's trained nose, it smelled like a scam of some sort. But what was the scam? If those elderly folks had handed over their heirlooms to Doug Hall—*why*?

"I'm sorry, Richard," Bly said. "I don't see anything here that helps us with your father."

"It helps," Hounslow said as he stood up.

"How?"

"That's what I'm about to find out."

CHAPTER 22

Somewhere over a very dark Frederick, Maryland, Malcolm's plane engines roared. Malcolm stared vacantly into the night sky. Jeff was buckled into the passenger seat, doing a balancing act with the many pages contained in the two reports they'd been given by Detective White. A tiny reading lamp splashed yellow on the papers.

"What are you doing?" Malcolm asked above the plane noise.

"Just killing time. I thought something might jump out at me if I looked long enough," Jeff replied. "Do you have any ideas about what's going on?"

"I have plenty of theories," Malcolm said, "but nothing I can call a good idea."

"Same here."

"Let's think crazy for a little while, okay?" Malcolm suggested. Thinking crazy, for Malcolm and Jeff, was a common exercise. It meant letting go of conventional ideas and considering the implausible—even the impossible.

"First, let's allow that Fawlt Line really is sitting on some kind of time fault. That's how Elizabeth slipped through. So did King Arthur. Maybe Adam did, too. But there's a problem."

"What kind of problem?" Jeff asked.

"According to Sheriff Hounslow, everything indicates that Adam went through *on purpose*. Detective White said essentially the same thing about McInery and Finney. It's as if their disappearances weren't an accident at all. They were planned. But how—and why?"

"I thought that's what we were trying to figure out," Jeff observed.

"It is. But to get the right answers, we have to come up with the right questions. So . . . what if all these missing people planned to disappear?"

Jeff turned another couple of pages. "Then I have to wonder where they disappeared *to*. Is it some scheme to give them new identities and false passports so they can all sunbathe in Latin America somewhere?"

"Maybe. But why did they all disappear in historical sites? And why did they sell their personal belongs to the shops from which they disappeared?"

"I give up. Why?"

"Beats me."

They flew on in silence for a while. Jeff continued to rifle through the pages, checking and double-checking bits of information.

Malcolm sighed. "I can't believe that Adam Hounslow is sunbathing in Latin America. It doesn't make sense. To go to all this trouble, someone like Adam Hounslow would want to go somewhere completely different. Somewhere that would do more than just let him escape."

"Like where?"

"If you were elderly, where would you want to go?" Malcolm asked.

Jeff thought about it for a minute. "If I were old and could go anywhere—anywhere at all—I'd probably want to go somewhere that would make me feel young again."

"Yes!" Malcolm shouted. "Of course you would! You'd want to go back in time to being a young man!"

"We *are* talking crazy."

"That's the idea of this exercise," Malcolm said. "What if Adam Hounslow figured out how to slip through time *on purpose*? What if he found a door, a way to go back through the time fault? Is that why he surrounded himself with his personal heirlooms? Were they the key to open the door somehow?"

Jeff scratched his head, "Okay. I'll play along. I can understand something like that happening in Fawlt Line because Fawlt Line is weird. But Boston? Baltimore? Annapolis?"

"Historic towns with historic buildings. Maybe people like

McInery and Finney figured out how to open the doors to other times in those old buildings, just as Adam Hounslow did."

"I can't believe that so many people would figure out a trick like that," Jeff said.

"Maybe *they* didn't figure it out. Maybe that's where Doug Hall fits in."

Jeff shook his head. "Doug Hall's only a little older than I am. How could he come up with an idea like that?"

"I was only a kid when I started thinking about time travel."

"Yeah, but thinking about time travel is one thing, actually figuring out how to do it is another. I can't believe that Doug—" Jeff suddenly stopped himself. A chill went up and down his spine.

Malcolm glanced over at his nephew. "What's wrong?"

Jeff was staring at the sheets on his lap. "Incredible."

"What?"

"Doug Hall didn't do it alone," Jeff said softly.

Malcolm couldn't hear him over the hum of the plane's engine. "What did you say?"

Jeff spoke louder. "There's a list of people here who were living at the Arundel Nursing Home where Doug worked."

"And?"

"George Betterman was there, too."

CHAPTER 13

At a quarter to ten, Elizabeth was idly pacing around Malcolm's den. She pulled one or two books from the shelves, glanced at them, put them back. Mrs. Packer had fallen asleep in front of the TV. Had the housekeeper remembered to call the security guard at the Village? In fifteen minutes, *something* was going to happen at the Fawlt Line Cinema. Would the guard check it out?

Maybe nothing would happen at all. Maybe Frieda Schultz's note wasn't a cryptic cry for help, but just an innocent reminder to herself—like a shopping or a "to do" list.

Maybe.

Elizabeth gazed at the sleeping Mrs. Packer, who was snoring softly.

I wish Jeff and Uncle Malcolm would hurry up and get back. Then they could go investigate the cinema together. But they wouldn't be back in time. No way. And there might not be anything to investigate anyway.

But every instinct in Elizabeth's body said that Mrs. Schultz's note was a cry for help. She was trying to tell them that something important was going to take place at ten o'clock this very night.

Elizabeth took a step toward the sleeping figure. "Mrs. Packer?" she said softly.

The housekeeper didn't stir.

Why wake her up? Elizabeth asked herself. The cinema was less than a mile away. She knew the path to get there—straight across the meadow and through the woods. She and Jeff had walked it a hundred times. She even knew how to open the private door Malcolm had put in the fence. Jeff had shown her. So why not go? What could be safer than the Village? She'd just slip in to see if anything was going on at the cinema and then slip out again.

With a final glance at Mrs. Packer, she opened the door to the patio and sneaked out.

The Fawlt Line Cinema—with a marquee announcing the premiere of *It Happened One Night*—was situated on an unfinished street that would eventually be dedicated to the 1930s. It was dark and deserted. For a moment, Elizabeth felt as if she had slipped through a different kind of fault and wound up in a gangster movie. She shivered and paused a few yards from the cinema's front door.

If something was going on, walking through the front door wouldn't be a smart thing to do. An alley ran to the back of the cinema. She followed it to the back door. It was unlocked. Wincing, she turned the handle carefully so as not to make a lot of noise. It creaked defiantly. Elizabeth got it open wide enough to slip through into a gray darkness. Dull red safety lights were on, giving off enough of a glow for her to see that she was in a hallway. An excited voice—like that of someone giving a lecture—echoed in another part of the building. Elizabeth tiptoed up the hall and toward the voice.

A light through a break in the wall caught her eye. She peeked through and saw that she was alongside the stage curtain with the movie screen. Beyond the edge of the stage, a group of people she recognized from the retirement center sat in a semicircle under a bald light, facing George Betterman in his wheelchair.

So, it was a "secret meeting" after all, she thought as her heart beat faster. George Betterman gestured wildly as he spoke. Obviously, he was the leader of this little club. She felt relieved to be proven right in her suspicions, but it didn't comfort her. It meant only that he was probably as dangerous as she always thought he was.

Elizabeth crept up the hallway until she came to a flight of stairs and an old sign with an arrow that said "Balcony." It would be a perfect vantage point to hear what he was saying, she thought, and cautiously climbed the stairs.

Her father was right about the cinema. Even though it wasn't completely set up, it was an ornate affair with thick curtains, tassels, and gold trimming that adorned the walls with swirling patterns. Elizabeth crawled along the dust-laden floor, through the unattached, disheveled chairs, to the edge of the balcony. On her knees, she slowly peeked over the railing, the smell of old wood in her nostrils. The balcony gave her a perfect view with an angle that let her see Betterman and his group, but they couldn't see her unless they were purposefully looking for her. She could hear George more clearly now as his voice echoed powerfully around her.

"We've all been waiting years for this!" he said. "Gone are the days of praying for a miracle—for those impossible, near perfect circumstances for us to travel. No more sneaking around old haunts, buildings, and shops. Malcolm Dubbs has given us the perfect passage. Fawlt Line is the perfect place at the perfect time!"

Betterman spoke like a preacher. Even though he was hunched in the wheelchair, wearing the oversized hat, sunglasses, and loose jogging suit, his voice and gesturing made him seem younger.

"Tonight is the night of miracles. Tonight all our hard work and sacrifice will be fulfilled. The words are on your lips, the keys are in your hands . . . the door to a better place awaits. Tonight you will reclaim your lost youth. Now you can say good-bye to twisted, arthritic bodies, ravaged by age. Return to your best days, your best health!"

Elizabeth tried to imagine how men and women so old and wise could believe such hype. Yet there they were: a small, elderly group who sat like wide-eyed children beholding a magician.

"Are there doubters?" he challenged them. "Then learn from Adam Hounslow! Where do you think he disappeared to? He believed, and now he is there! Do you need more case histories? Look at the files and names I showed you. Where do you think they went? They went back to their youth—their paradise. The police couldn't find them. How could they?"

Elizabeth closed her eyes. What was he saying? Adam Hounslow went back in time? Had George Betterman figured out how to send people back in time to better days? Was it possible?

"This is my gift to you," he said gently. "I spent every day of every year of my life in this time to piece it all together. Even while many called me insane. Even when they called me an amnesiac. I kept the faith. I knew who I was!"

Her skin crawled, and she wrapped her arms around herself to fight the uneasy feeling that was growing inside of her. *No, it can't be.* He was saying the same things she said when she was trapped in that other time. They said she was insane. They said she was an amnesiac. And she had to cling to the belief that she wasn't someone called Sarah. She was Elizabeth. She clenched her fists at the memory. *I am Elizabeth.*

Again, she saw George Betterman in her dream. *I know who you are*, he had said. *Sarah.*

Betterman's tone built to a fevered pitch. "They had no idea, those fools. I knew that other times existed. I knew that there was a way to get back. But this was my purgatory, I realized. It doesn't have to be yours! There is a way out, and I will now help you if you will believe. Adam made it out! Now you will too!" He pointed at them. "Are there any doubters now? Are there? Well, if you won't believe my words—if you won't believe the testimony of Adam—then believe this!"

Elizabeth's heart stopped, and the small group gasped collectively George Betterman leapt to his feet and victoriously pushed the wheelchair aside. Elizabeth grabbed the railing to steady herself. *He can walk! The wheelchair was a fake!*

A buzz went through the group. But Betterman wasn't finished with his presentation. "Tonight we strip away the facades, we rid ourselves of these feeble outer garments. Tonight we become our true selves!"

With one hand he grabbed his hat and slid it off. The wild hair came with it to reveal short salt-and-pepper colored hair. Elizabeth's eyes grew wider as a picture she'd been trying to form in her mind started taking shape. Salt-and-pepper hair. So familiar.

Then he pulled off his beard and mustache. Then the sunglasses. And he tilted his face toward the light and laughed like a younger man.

Elizabeth put both fists against her mouth to stifle the scream rising in her throat. The picture was complete. She now knew why she recognized him. It was Charles Richards.

She stumbled backward, narrowly grabbing a chair before it toppled.

"Go now!" he commanded them like Moses dismissing the children of Israel. "You know what to do! Go to your destiny!"

Elizabeth fought back the tears and tried to calm her palpitating heart.

No, it wasn't Charles Richards. *It couldn't be*, her overloaded mind told her. Charles Richards was a good man. He'd saved her life. He wouldn't have returned to this time to become so evil. No, it looked like Charles Richards, but it wasn't.

Her brain nearly seized up as she tried to sort through the hows and whys. Just as Sarah was her time-twin, George Betterman must be the time-twin for Charles Richards. It had to be! Charles was trapped in the other time, but his twin—no one knew what had become of him.

Elizabeth took several deep breaths to calm herself. She had to call someone—anyone. It wasn't right. Did those poor misguided old people really understand what they were doing or where they were going? How could Betterman be sure of where he was sending them? They had to be stopped. Elizabeth had to get out of there and tell somebody!

She quickly crawled back to the doorway to the hall and stood up.

Doug Hall stepped out of the shadows.

"Hello, Elizabeth." He smiled. "Or should I call you Sarah?"

"Does the phrase 'obstruction of justice' mean anything to you?" Sheriff Hounslow snarled at Mrs. Kottler. He had driven straight to the retirement center from the boarding house in Grantsville. Along the way, he received a message from Malcolm Dubbs that George Betterman was definitely linked to the case and needed to be detained.

"Please, Sheriff," Mrs. Kottler said, moving in front of him as they walked quickly down the hallway. "The residents are traumatized as it is. Can't you wait until morning? You'll wake everyone up!"

"Waking some of them up is exactly what I have in mind—starting with George Betterman! Now get out of my way."

She hovered in front of him. "I have to insist that—"

Hounslow stopped in his tracks. "Bob!"

Deputy Peterson, who'd been trying to keep up, joined them. "Yes, sir?" he panted.

"Get her out of my way," he said.

"Yes, sir." With surprising speed and strength, the deputy grabbed Mrs. Kottler's wrist.

"Now, wait just a minute—" Mrs. Kottler protested.

"If she causes any trouble, arrest her!" Hounslow shouted as he continued down the hall.

It didn't take him very long to realize that he was on a wild goose chase. Betterman wasn't in his room, nor were the other ten people who had sold their belongings through Doug Hall.

"Where are they?" Sheriff Hounslow demanded when he returned from his search.

Mrs. Kottler blinked innocently. "Aren't they in their rooms?"

Hounslow pointed a finger at her. "Mrs. Kottler, I hope you're not involved in this. If I find out you that are, I'll throw the book at you."

She cleared her throat nervously. "Now that you mention it . . . I believe some of the residents decided to take a drive in the center van. They do that sometimes, you know. I think George Betterman may have been among them. And who else were you looking for?"

"Mrs. Kottler," the sheriff said in a low growl. "You'd better tell me *now* where they went. And then I suggest you call your lawyer."

CHAPTER 15

Doug Hall tore a strip of tassel from the stage curtain and tied Elizabeth's hands behind her back. She struggled until George Betterman slapped her. The sting brought tears to her eyes.

"I'm sorry, Sarah," Betterman said in earnest. "But if you don't behave, we're going to have a real problem on our hands."

Except for the three of them, the cinema was now empty. The retirement center residents had gone on to do whatever it was they came to the Village to do.

"I'm not Sarah," Elizabeth said.

Betterman smiled sympathetically at her. "You don't have to play that game with me. I know who you really are. You're Sarah Bishop. I knew your family in the *real* Fawlt Line—across the chasm of time. Your father and I grew up together. You look a lot like your mother, actually."

Elizabeth winced as Doug gave the tassel a final tug to make sure it was secure. "You didn't know my family. You knew Sarah's. Haven't you figured it out? She's my time-twin. Just like you have a time-twin that you switched with when you came over. I met him. His name was Charles Richards and—"

"Shut up!" he shouted. "I don't want to hear this . . . this heresy. Do you think I've spent my life here in vain? I *know* what happened to me. And I know what will happen tonight."

"Do you really? Do you have any idea where you're sending those people?"

"To paradise," he said.

Elizabeth scowled at him. "Or to the *other* Fawlt Line— where they'll be locked away as insane amnesiacs. Just like I was. Just like you were when you got here! They'll still be old. They won't be any happier. Why would you do that to them?"

"What you don't know is a lot," he said with a chuckle. "They have the incantations, they have their trinkets. This is the pinnacle of time transference—to go to the places of their dreams where they will find youth and happiness again. Gone are the aches and pains of age. In these buildings, generously assembled by Malcolm Dubbs, they will stand at the doorway to time, say the words I've given to them, offer the meager souvenirs we've already cleverly placed for them, and then step through."

"To what?" Elizabeth asked as she imagined the residents moving like zombies through the Village to their assigned buildings, their doorways. "Step through to what? Only God knows what's out there! You don't. You *can't*. Not all doors lead to a better place! Please, Mr. Betterman, stop them."

Betterman wagged a finger at her. "Oh, don't be such a doubter, Sarah. They'll go to a better place—or die trying." He laughed again.

At that moment, Elizabeth knew she was dealing with a madman.

"In fact," he said, "you and I should also make that trip across time. What do you say, Sarah? Shall we go home now?"

"No!" Elizabeth cried out, then screamed as Doug Hall lifted her to her feet. "No!"

Malcolm phoned Mrs. Packer as soon as he and Jeff landed at the Fawlt Line Airport. The first thing he learned was that Elizabeth was missing.

He put his hand over the receiver and turned to Jeff. "Elizabeth left the cottage and didn't go home. Any idea where she might be?"

Jeff's mouth fell open. "What time did she leave?"

Malcolm asked Mrs. Packer, then turned back to Jeff. "Around ten o'clock."

"I'll bet she's in the Village—at the old cinema."

Malcolm looked puzzled. "Why would she . . . ?" Then he remembered. "Mrs. Schultz's note! We're on our way."

He listened to Mrs. Packer again, then groaned. "Call security again right away and see if they've found anything . . . You didn't?! . . . Just call them *now*, Mrs. Packer. I'll think about firing you later. Also, call Donald Nelson and tell him I'll meet him at the front gate. He knows what it's about."

Malcolm hung up the phone and moved quickly toward the jeep.

"What's going on?" Jeff demanded.

"Everything. And I'm afraid Elizabeth's in the middle of it. Mrs. Packer said Hounslow called five minutes ago and said he was going to the Village. Something to do with George Betterman."

Donald Nelson was waiting for Malcolm and Jeff when they screeched to a halt at the front gate of the Village.

"Hello, Donald," Malcolm said as he climbed out of the jeep. "Where is everyone?"

Donald rolled his eyes. "Sheriff Hounslow came in with his guns ablaze, barking orders at everybody in sight. He sent his men and all the security guards to search the Village for George Betterman and Doug Hall."

"They're both here?" Jeff asked.

"Hounslow seems to think so. I believe he persuaded a Mrs. Kottler to confess, and she said—"

Jeff pressed his hand against his forehead. "Mrs. Kottler's in on this?"

"I'm only telling you what I heard."

"I'm going to the cinema," Jeff announced, then ran off.

Malcolm turned to Donald. "Did you do what I asked?"

"As best as I could in the time I had."

"Good enough. Let's go." Malcolm strode into the Village.

Jeff was nearly tackled and shot three times by police and security guards as he raced through the Village to the cinema. He shouted where he was going and why and, before he knew it, had five men running with him. When they reached the cinema, the door was standing open and Hounslow was already inside.

"They aren't here," the sheriff said from the center of the auditorium. In his hand he held a wig, cap, sunglasses, and a beard. "I assume this is what's left of George Betterman."

"Have you seen Elizabeth? Has *anyone* seen Elizabeth?" Jeff asked anxiously.

Hounslow shook his head, then yanked the walkie-talkie from his belt and asked for a report from around the Village.

Deputy Peterson informed him that they'd rounded up half a dozen folks from the retirement center, but they hadn't seen Elizabeth. He also said they had found a service-entrance gate unlocked and open.

"That's how the center van got in—and probably out again," Hounslow said.

"Then where did they go? They have Elizabeth with them!" Jeff said.

Hounslow clicked the button on his walkie-talkie. "Okay, guys, keep searching the Village, but I want a detail of men to hit the road. That retirement center van is headed somewhere, and I want it found. It's likely the suspects have Elizabeth Forde with them. And somebody get me a helicopter from the Frostburg police!"

Jeff dashed out of the building.

Hounslow looked at his officers. "What were all those old folks doing here? What kind of game were they playing?"

His men looked back at him without answering.

Malcolm and Donald cautiously stepped into the dimly lit farmhouse. It was on the outer edge of the Village and had been built to capture a lifestyle known to most midwestern farmers from the turn-of-the-century.

"Hello?" Malcolm called out.

His voice echoed throughout the house.

"You're sure this was one of them?" Malcolm asked Donald.

"Positive," he answered. "Doug Hall sold several boxes of things on behalf of the Sawyer family. They were designated for this house. I believe the Sawyers were farmers when—"

Malcolm held up a hand for him to be quiet. He had heard a noise in the next room. Now Donald heard it, too. It was the sound of a man whimpering. Malcolm turned on a light in what would have once been a family room. Tiffany lamps, wing-backed chairs, full bookcases, a player piano sat atop a deep red Persian carpet. A wizened old man sat in the corner, half-hidden by an end table and one of the chairs.

"Mr. Sawyer?" Malcolm said softly. "Are you all right?"

The man wept uncontrollably, his face buried in his hands. "They're not here."

"What's not here?"

"My *things*," he sobbed. "They were supposed to be here. How can I go back if they aren't here? I've said the words over and over again, but they're no good without my things."

"I had Mr. Nelson collect all of your things, Mr. Sawyer. He collected the belongings of everyone from the retirement center."

"But why?" the old man pleaded. "Don't you see? I can't go back without them. It won't work. Don't you understand? Please bring them back. George promised that I'd go through time if I had my things and said the words."

Malcolm and Donald exchange a sad look. "George is a liar, Mr. Sawyer," Malcolm said.

"No . . . he can't be. We all believed him. He sent Adam back. He could do the same for us. He promised."

"How much did you all pay George for his little promise?" Malcolm asked.

The old man looked up at him helplessly and confessed, "All we had."

CHAPTER 27

A police car flew past with its lights flashing and siren screaming.

"All clear?" George Betterman asked.

Doug leaned forward to check the road in both directions. "All clear." He started up the motor and guided the van back on to the road.

George turned in the passenger seat and addressed Elizabeth, who was tied up and stretched out on the floor of the van. "It won't be long now," he murmured.

She grunted through the duct tape over her mouth.

Doug turned onto an unpaved road. The van bounced its way along, and Elizabeth grunted and groaned with each bump.

"I liked your family, Sarah," George said. "Good people. I thought of them a lot when I came to this time. They were some of the folks I missed. So you can imagine my surprise when I found out that you were here too. I was delighted. Wasn't I delighted, Doug?"

"You were," Doug replied.

George Betterman turned to face her again. "Ever since I got here, I've been studying time travel and weird phenomena. It was sort of a natural interest to me since I'd come from another time. Nobody believed me, though. They just wanted to lock me up and throw away the key. In fact, Doug here was the only one who believed me. We were at that Happy Dale Sanitarium, weren't we?"

Doug nodded. "Uh-huh."

"It was Doug who happened to see a teeny-tiny article in some cheesy tabloid about the mysterious disappearance of a girl in a strange little town called Fawlt Line. She disappeared right out of her bathtub, the article said. Then the writer pointed out that this was the same Fawlt Line where several other bizarre things had happened over the last fifty years. That tabloid writer meant it as a joke, I know, but it sure got my interest. Do you remember, Doug?"

"I remember." Doug smiled. "It was all you talked about."

"I thought, well, we're going to have to check out old Fawlt Line and those bizarre occurrences. It took some doing."

"A lot of money," Doug put in.

"That's right. I got a couple of interns at the hospital to tell me everything they knew about the girl in a coma who was supposed to be Elizabeth, but wasn't. And later I heard things about her disappearing right under the doctor's nose. Then a rookie cop who has since gone on to better things told me about all the other peculiar things that happened. He even got me a classified file from the police station that had a full statement from you and Jeff and Malcolm. And as soon as I read the name Sarah Bishop, I knew. I put two and two together and knew that you were Sarah— only they'd brainwashed you into believing you were Elizabeth. Better than that, I realized that Fawlt Line was the town for me!"

A tear slid down Elizabeth's nose and onto the worn carpet.

Doug brought the van to a halt and got out. George climbed back to help Elizabeth sit up. "Your father would be proud of how you turned out," he said.

Doug opened the side door to the van, and George guided Elizabeth out. She hit the gravel on wobbly knees and looked around for anything that might tell her where they were.

They had brought her to the Old Sawmill.

"Great idea, huh?" Doug said.

"If I remember right, this is where you and Jeff suddenly showed up after all your switching back and forth through time. So we figured it would be the best place for what we need to do. Didn't we, Doug?"

"Yep," Doug said.

George smiled at her. "You've done me no end of good, Sarah. You and Malcolm. You're inspirations to me. I thought I had died and gone to heaven when I heard he was building his historic village. It was as if he'd done it just for me. I thought: here's a man with vision. A whole village with doorways into time. Perfect, absolutely perfect. Take that tape off her mouth, will you, Doug?"

Doug gently removed the tape. "Is that better?"

"Yes," Elizabeth said breathlessly. "What are we doing here? Why are we at the Old Sawmill?"

"You'll see," George said, as he and Doug each took an elbow and escorted Elizabeth into the derelict wooden building. It was full of cobwebs and the smell of rotting wood and sawdust. Somewhere, not far beyond the woods, they could hear a river splashing over the rocks.

"Memories, huh?" Doug said.

Elizabeth remembered, all right, and it sent a shiver of panic through her entire body. She had sworn to herself that she would never come back here. Not only because of what had happened before, but because of what she feared could happen again. Now it seemed as if George was going to *make* it happen.

She struggled against her captors. "I don't want to be here. Take me away from here."

George clicked his tongue at her. "Now don't fuss, Sarah. This is all for the best."

"I'm not Sarah!" Elizabeth shouted at him. "I'm Elizabeth! Sarah is in the other time where she belongs. I'm in this time where I belong! Cross over if you know how to, but don't take me with you!"

"Oh, now, you have to at least try," George said. "How will we know if it really works unless we experiment on you? If you cross over, then maybe Doug and I can too."

"You and Doug?" Elizabeth asked, bewildered. "It doesn't work that way."

"It has to. What would I go back to, if Doug doesn't come with me? My wife has probably married someone else. My kids will be grown up with kids of their own. Doug here is the only family I have now."

"But what about my family? My life?"

"What about them? Good grief, Sarah, you haven't been here

that long." George signaled to Doug. "Tie her to the pole."

Doug pulled Elizabeth to a supporting pole in the center of the mill. He brought a stretch of cord out of his back pocket and secured her already tied wrists to the beam.

Elizabeth glared at Doug. "It won't work if I'm tied up."

He kissed her on the cheek. "You're a clever girl. If I untie you, you'll figure out how to run away." Once he was certain she was secure, he turned to George. "What now?"

"Let's say the words and see what happens."

"You're kidding."

"What have we got to lose? If it's going to work for anybody, it'll work for her."

"If you insist . . ." Doug stepped away from Elizabeth and stood next to George. They faced her for a moment, then closed their eyes.

"Please don't do this," Elizabeth said.

George raised his arms. "Force of Time, Endless River, Open Door."

"I don't want to be sent to another time. Please, don't!"

"In Time there is regeneration and rebirth," George continued. "We seek it within ourselves. We seek it within Time. Send now the Force of Time to take Sarah to her happiest time. Through the Force of Time, take her into that doorway. Take her . . . and may the Force be with her."

Elizabeth stared at George incredulously.

Doug chuckled. "May the Force be with her?"

George shrugged. "It seemed like the right thing to say. The old folks always liked it."

"Is this some kind of cruel joke?" Elizabeth asked angrily.

George pondered the question. "Cruel? Maybe. A joke? Hardly. You see, I really do believe in time travel, but I've never been able to figure out how to master it. It's been an endless source of disappointment."

"Then what was all that 'crossing over' stuff?"

"You're going to cross over, all right," George explained.

"But not in the way you expected. In a manner of speaking, you're going to join Adam."

"Adam? Adam Hounslow? Where is he?"

Doug hooked a thumb toward another part of the mill. "He's under a tarp in the back."

"Go get the boxes, Doug," George said, and the younger man obeyed.

Elizabeth's mouth was agape. "You mean, Adam didn't go to another time? He's . . . he's . . . you killed him?"

"We didn't kill him. It was an accident. See, the plan was supposed to be simple. Adam would send his son off on some errand, then go into the miners' row house where he thought he'd say the words and disappear to Never-Never Land. He was my proof to the other old folks that what I was saying was true. Well, we put up a quick 'Do Not Enter' sign on the front of the row house, used a little chloroform, dropped Adam into my wheelchair and dressed him up to look like me. Of course, then nobody recognized me without cap, sunglasses, and a lot of hair, so I just walked out. That's how I got the dirt and grass on my shoes. It was Doug who had buried Adam's stuff the night before."

Doug had returned with some boxes and listened to George's recounting of their tale. He turned to Elizabeth. "You'll forgive me for not saying hello when we were leaving the Village. I was afraid you might want to make conversation and realize that the man in the wheelchair wasn't George."

"The plan was to bring Adam here and keep him locked up until we got the rest of the money from the old fogies at the center," George said.

"Quite a coup, getting the sheriff's father to buy into the scheme," Doug said proudly. "It gave us a lot of credibility with the doubters."

"What happened to him?" Elizabeth asked.

"Doug brought him here, but to our surprise, he had died en route. Maybe we gave him too much chloroform, or it triggered a heart attack or something. Sad. Same thing happened to Frieda

Schultz. I wanted to scare her enough to keep her mouth shut, and she started wailing like a banshee. Her heart gave out. It just wasn't our week, was it, Doug?"

Elizabeth shook her head. "So the whole thing was a scam."

"Not just a scam," George protested. "A great scam. We've been doing it all over the country. Besides, what's wrong with giving old folks a little hope in their dreary lives?"

"Plenty, when people get murdered or—"

George held up a hand. "All right, all right. Don't get preachy. It's a risk of the trade and small compensation for the life *I* lost when I switched from my time to this one. Anyway, it was nice while it lasted."

"While it lasted?"

"This was our last hurrah," he said. "Doug and I are moving on to greener pastures. Aren't we, Doug?"

Doug had left and then returned with another couple of boxes. "Uh-huh. This is the last of it."

"What happens now?" Elizabeth asked.

George flicked his hand at the boxes. "Oh, these boxes have all the evidence about our little program. By the time the police find you and Adam and the boxes, we'll be long gone."

"South America," Doug added. "I've been learning Spanish."

Elizabeth scowled. "You're just going to leave me here?"

"Yes, my dear," George said. "What happens to you from this point forward isn't my concern. Good-bye." He walked out.

Doug leaned close to her face. His breath smelled of mint. "We could have made beautiful music together," he said, brushing his lips against hers. "*Buenos noches.*"

"Don't leave me here like this!" Elizabeth called after him. "Please!"

Doug climbed into the van, started the engine, put it into gear, then jumped out again to watch as the van propelled itself over the embankment and down into the woods. It crashed head-on against a tree and died. He then ran over to a small blue car where George was waiting in the passenger seat. "Ready?" he asked.

George scrubbed his chin. "I don't like it, leaving her there. What if they find everything before we get out of the country?"

"Good point."

"You better take care of it."

Doug got out of the car. He went around to the trunk and pulled out a gas can, then walked to one of the mill's walls and splashed the liquid on the sides. He lit a match and placed it against the wood. It went up fast.

Back in the car, he said, "That old dry wood will be gone in no time at all."

George smiled and cocked an ear to something he heard in the sky above. "I'm sure you're right. Let's get out of here."

CHAPTER 28

Fred Danziger, a helicopter pilot from the Frostburg police, had been watching the road for a white van. The call came in as he was just ending his shift to go home. He was tired and annoyed and muttered curses at Sheriff Hounslow, Fawlt Line, and whatever bad guys down there had started the kind of trouble that required his services. "Watch for a white passenger van with printing on the side," was all he knew.

Small towns, he snorted to himself. *What happened? Did somebody steal Grandma's quilt?* Route 40 was clear. So was the bypass. He circled around and saw a glimmer of moonlight reflect off the small river below. He couldn't remember the river's name—or if it even had one. He had a vague notion that it was once used for mining or lumber mills.

He yawned, then did a double take as he realized that the moonlight on the river had taken on a red-and-yellow glow. It wasn't moonlight at all. It was the reflection of a fire that seemed to be working its way up the side of a large wooden building. A mill, he guessed. He hit the spotlight to confirm that the building really was on fire.

Another pinprick of light caught his eye, and he trained the spotlight on the road running away from the mill. A small blue car was speeding recklessly away from the scene.

Fred grabbed his radio microphone.

CHAPTER 29

Elizabeth twisted around to see if there was any way to undo the knots on her wrists or the pole. Doug had done a thorough job. He was probably a world-class boy scout, she thought. Her hands were going to sleep.

She suddenly stopped and sniffed the air. The thick smoke that curled ribbonlike through the cracks in the wall told her all she needed to know.

She screamed, but knew there was no one around to help her.

Twisting and squirming until her arms and back ached, she worked her wrists back and forth. The rope and cord cut through her skin. She twisted her head around to get a clearer view of how she'd been tied up. Double, even triple knots had her securely bound.

The fire hissed and crackled outside. Something shifted above her. She was horrified to realize that the flames had moved to the roof. The smoke was thicker inside now. Elizabeth coughed.

She looked down again at the ropes, the cord, the pole, to see if there was anything at all that might set her free. *God, help me*, she prayed. *Help me*.

She spotted part of a nail sticking out of the pole, just a few inches beneath her bonds. Using all of her weight, she pushed downward, hoping to catch the ropes or the cords on the nail itself. Maybe if she rubbed back and forth enough, the nail would fray the ropes enough so she could break free. She'd seen heroes do it on television. The ropes cut into her wrists more as she pressed down with all of her might. Beads of sweat appeared on her forehead. The feeling was completely gone from her hands. She coughed harder as the smoke poured in.

I won't burn to death, she thought glibly. *The smoke will kill me first*.

Suddenly she wished that she *could* transfer to another time.

137

It looked like her only escape.

The fire was wildly alive now, and pieces of wood were falling down from the roof. Elizabeth frantically scraped the ropes against the rusted nail. Her eyes teared up, and her coughing became more violent. *How long will it take?* she wondered as her struggle with the nail dwindled. She had a different struggle now: the struggle to stay conscious.

Oh, God, somebody must have seen the flames. Somebody must be on their way. But will they make it in time?

She put all of her strength into another jerk at the ropes and the nail. Then another. Then another. Blackness closed in, and she slumped against the pole. Her legs gave out, and the tightness of the ropes twisted her arms agonizingly upward, but she didn't notice.

She was barely conscious when a figure moved ghostlike across the floor. It came toward her through the smoke.

CHAPTER 30

Fred Danziger's radio report brought instant reaction. All the local fire engines were sent screaming to the Old Sawmill. Hounslow ordered the helicopter to stay on the mysterious blue car until he and his men could intercept it further down Route 40. Roadblocks were immediately set up. The chase was on.

"Faster, faster!" Hounslow shouted at his car. In the distance, he could see the blue car's taillights. The helicopter suddenly swooped in, washing the scene in white light. "Okay, that's it. Let's drive the fox to the hounds."

Doug Hall swore and pounded the steering wheel. "It's not fair! It's not fair!"

"Just keep driving, son," George Betterman said as he glanced back at the red-and-blue lights coming toward them in the darkness. The spotlight from the helicopter suddenly hit them again in a blinding flash. "We'll think of something."

"Roadblock!" Doug shouted.

George jerked around. The line of police cars with their flashing lights was unmistakable. They were about a hundred yards ahead.

"What should we do? I can't ram them in this little match-box," Doug said.

George considered their options to the left and the right. The woods were thick on both sides. "We can make a run for it. Hit the brakes," he said.

Doug began to slow down. "Are you sure?"

Hounslow's siren got louder as it came up behind them.

"I didn't say to slow down! I said *hit the brakes*!" With that, George lifted his foot and slammed it down on top of Doug's on the brake pedal. The car screeched as the brakes locked and the car went into a skid.

Hounslow swore as he slammed on his brakes.

The car ahead swerved to the left, then skidded in a half circle. It spun another few degrees and turned onto its side. Hounslow had a clear view of the undercarriage as it careened toward the gully that lined the right side of the road. Sparks flew, metal shrieked. Off the pavement, the car hit the dirt and then flipped upside down at the edge of the woods.

Hounslow's vehicle also threatened to swerve as he wrestled for control. The antilocking mechanism kicked in and brought the car to a sensible halt amidst the smell of burning rubber and smoke.

The sheriff shouted into his radio microphone. "Did you see that? Get an ambulance down here right away!" He leapt out of the car and raced to the tangled blue mess that now looked like an upside-down turtle in the ditch. The turn signal flashed forlornly, like an appeal for help. The helicopter seemed to appear from nowhere, its spotlight illuminating the scene starkly.

Doug Hall pulled himself out of the car. "George! George!" he called in a dazed voice. A thick line of red appeared on his forehead and sent drops of blood down his nose and cheeks.

George Betterman was on the passenger side where the car met the slant of the gully. "I'm trapped," George gasped as Doug stumbled around to him.

Hounslow reached the two of them with his gun in hand. "Don't move," he commanded.

"I don't think I can," Betterman said as a tiny sliver of blood trickled from the corner of his mouth. "I seem to have lost the feeling in my legs."

"We'll get you out, George. Don't worry," Doug said. "They're all coming to help."

George chuckled and coughed. "Wouldn't that be a kick? All these years faking it in a wheelchair—now I might have to do it for real."

Doug let out a dry sob. "Don't think about that, George. It'll be all right."

As the helicopter trained its spotlight on them and the rest of the police cars pulled up, Hounslow looked down at the two men with steely eyes. "Where is my father?" he asked.

Len Sebastian, Fawlt Line's fire chief, put his hands on his hips and watched the Old Sawmill tilt like a storm-tossed ship and collapse in a sea of fire. "We should've torn this place down years ago," he muttered to himself.

His squad of firemen blasted water at the flames from three different hoses.

"Chief! Hounslow's on the horn for you!" somebody shouted.

Sebastian leaned into his car and grabbed the radio. "Sebastian here."

"It's Hounslow. Did you find anybody?"

"Find anybody where?" he asked.

"In the Old Sawmill? Were there any survivors?"

Sebastian looked at the flaming wreckage. His years of experience said that if anyone was inside, he couldn't have survived. "Well, Sheriff—"

He was interrupted by a shout. "Chief! Yo—Chief!"

"Hold on," Sebastian said. His man pointed toward the woods.

"I'll get back to you," he said and dropped the microphone. He ran to the woods and pushed through a group of his men. Sitting next to a tree, covered in a protective fire jacket, a girl cried and coughed. Next to her lay an old man.

Someone leaned over to Sebastian and said, "He's alive, but just barely."

"Get an ambulance!" Sebastian snapped. He knelt next to the girl. "Can you talk?"

She nodded, then coughed and cleared her throat. "Yes," she rasped.

"Who are you?"

"Elizabeth Forde," she whispered. Tears formed rivulets

down her soot-stained cheeks.

There was another commotion in the crowd as Jeff, then Malcolm, pushed their way through.

"Bits!" Jeff cried out and stumbled to her.

She threw herself into her arms and lost whatever self-control was left. "He saved my life," she said through wrenching sobs and coughs.

"Who?"

"Adam Hounslow."

CHAPTER 31

"I thought I died," Adam Hounslow told his son in a thin voice. "It was like a dream."

He was on a stretcher in the back of the ambulance, speeding for the hospital. The sheriff sat next to him. He was suffering from malnutrition and dehydration, the paramedic had said. Some smoke inhalation, too. Adam coughed softly.

"For once in your life, be quiet," Hounslow said.

"Don't talk to your father like that," Adam replied. He was emaciated and looked at his son with sunken eyes. "What if I don't make it to the hospital?"

"It'd be just like you to do that to me." Hounslow half smiled.

Adam swallowed hard. "Then you should know now."

"Know what?"

"Betterman and that Hall kid sold us a load of nonsense. They got us all worked up about going to a better place in time."

"I know, Dad," Hounslow said. "We got the whole story from some of your pals at the center."

"I wanted it, Richard. I wanted another life. That's why I agreed to be their guinea pig. But when I got to the row house and they hit me with that chloroform, I knew it was a scam. I wanted to die right then and there. I didn't care anymore. To have hope— and lose it so quickly—was more than I could take."

"Calm down, will you?" Hounslow said soothingly and stroked his father's matted hair.

Adam sniffled. "It was like those other times. I went deep inside myself."

"A self-induced coma, I think the doctors called it," Hounslow suggested.

"Whatever. All I know is I felt an emptiness like I'd never felt before. It was horrible. But I thought that's what death was like, so I figured I really had died. It was like a dream. Then I started coughing and thought, 'Wait a minute, dead people don't cough.' So I opened my eyes and there I was, all wrapped up. I thought I was in a coffin, Richard. I thought I was buried alive." He went into a coughing fit.

"Take it easy!" Hounslow said and put a restraining hand on his father's arm. "You're giving me the creeps. Just lie still."

"That's when I realized that I didn't want to be dead," Adam went on, when he caught his breath again. "I wanted to live. So I punched a fist at the coffin lid, and it wasn't a coffin lid after all. It was a tarp. I fought my way out and saw that girl tied to the pole, and the building on fire, and there was no question about it. I wanted to live."

"You saved Elizabeth's life."

"Did I? Oh, well, that's nice."

Hounslow gazed at his father and saw a light in his eyes that he hadn't seen in a long time. It was *life*. "Dad . . ."

"Yeah?"

"I was thinking . . . maybe you should move in with me."

A thin smile crossed Adam's face. "What—are you kidding? And give up bingo at the center?"

Hounslow took his father's hand and laughed.

CHAPTER 32

The charred remains of the Old Sawmill seemed strangely peaceful under the blue morning sky. The twisted metal stairs leading to a second-floor office reminded Elizabeth of an abstract sculpture she'd once seen. The blackened door stood open on its hinges and the shell beyond sat like a stage waiting for a play to begin. Elizabeth shivered as a cool breeze swept through. She had come back to the site hoping to put a permanent end to this bad dream. She looked down at the bandages on her wrists. *Let it be over now*, she thought.

"Are you all right?" Jeff asked softly.

Elizabeth coughed, then cleared her throat. The doctor said she'd be doing a lot of that over the next few days. "As well as can be expected."

Malcolm suddenly appeared, stepping gingerly over the heap of rubble. He was wearing heavy boots and looked as though he should be fly-fishing, not walking around a burned-down building. "I found it!" he exclaimed and held something up.

A bird screeched indignantly from a tree nearby and flew off.

"What did you find?" Jeff called back to him.

Malcolm leapt from the last fallen beam and walked across the lot to them. "The ax Adam used to cut you loose, Elizabeth."

"Is that how he did it? I wasn't sure."

"I thought it'd be nice to have when we go visit him this afternoon."

Elizabeth looked thoughtfully at the wreckage. "I prayed for God to help me when I was inside there. I guess I expected him to make the ropes fall off. I didn't expect him to bring Adam Hounslow back."

Malcolm chuckled. "Looks like God answered two prayers. Yours and the sheriff's."

They stood in silence for a moment until Elizabeth coughed again. "Do you think it's over?"

Baffled, Jeff and Malcolm looked at her.

"Now that the Old Sawmill is gone, is the door closed to that other time?"

Malcolm shrugged. "I don't know. Can anybody know for sure? Only God knows, so it's enough for us to leave it to Him."

Elizabeth breathed deeply, wanting to believe it. "Right."

"Although . . ." Malcolm began, then paused.

"Although what?" Jeff asked.

"It makes me wonder about the Village."

"What about it?"

"Well, I've been thinking about George Betterman," Malcolm said. "Because of people like him, there are places in this world that can become centers of the wrong kinds of thinking—where the truth gets distorted into a terrible lie and false hope gets sold to the vulnerable. I built the Village as a testimony to history. Without realizing it, I may have opened new and very dangerous doors. That worries me. What's in the future for the Village, if it's going to become the center of things that are misguided and evil?"

"But that could happen anywhere, to anything," Jeff said.

Elizabeth cleared her throat and spoke quietly. "You always taught us that when people learn the truth, they're less susceptible to lies. Crooks like George Betterman and Doug Hall can only do what they do because people turn their backs on the truth. Isn't that how it works?"

Malcolm fixed his gaze on Elizabeth, pleased. "That's right. Sometimes we'll do just about anything when we're afraid, or we've lost hope, or we've forgotten how to appreciate our lives. But in God's truth, there is no fear. There's hope and life. Remembering that will always keep the George Bettermans in their place." Malcolm chuckled. "Time to step off my soapbox. The Village opens in fifteen minutes, and I need to be there."

He turned and walked to his jeep. Jeff took Elizabeth's hand and started to follow. She paused for a moment to look back at the skeletal remains of the Old Sawmill. The rubble, the twisted stairs, the shell of the office, and that door . . . she had a feeling about that door. No, not a feeling. A small prayer.

"What's wrong?" Jeff asked.

"Wait," she whispered.

A breeze gently blew the door closed.

She closed her eyes gratefully. "Now it's over," she said.

Here's what other readers are saying about Paul McCusker's Time Twists novels . . .

"This series is great. The plots are so exciting I could hardly put the books down."
—Erin D.

"The books are wonderful! I stayed up until five A.M. reading one because it was so exciting!"
—Katie S.

"Your novel made me think. It made me ask questions. You also painted a picture in my mind while I was reading."
—Natalie R.

"It was such an intriguing book I didn't even notice when I was turning the pages. The story has a good moral for kids.
—Philip B.

"The book was very adventurous. . . . When I get a good book like this one, I just can't put it down."
—Jacob A.

Here's a chapter from Time Twists 1, *Sudden Switch*

CHAPTER ■ 3 ■　　　　　　　　　# Sudden Switch

The funny thing was: Elizabeth didn't want to take a bath in the first place. But it seemed to be the only refuge for her frayed nerves. She was angry with Jeff for not agreeing wholeheartedly to run away with her. And once she returned to the Victorian house she called home, her folks seemed unusually attentive to her, as if they knew she was up to something. *It's that old "parents' radar" again, she thought. Somehow they know when they're not wanted and insist on staying close by.*

Her mother said she'd heard that Elizabeth and Jeff had had some sort of quarrel at the diner. How had that news reached home even before she did? Small towns were unbelievable . . . and Fawlt Line was surely among the worst. Her mother was concerned—she knew Elizabeth and Jeff never quarreled. Was everything all right, she wanted to know. Elizabeth mumbled a vague response and excused herself to go to her room.

She was looking in her closet for good running-away clothes when her mother came in. More questions. "Are you feeling all right? Are you sure you don't want to talk about what happened with Jeff? You seem unhappy about something, Elizabeth. What is it?"

Elizabeth ran out of evasive answers and finally

announced that she was going to take a bath. It was the only escape; the only reprieve for her tense muscles and tangled emotions.

As she stepped into the bathroom that adjoined her bedroom, Elizabeth turned to glance at her mother. "Your father and I have a meeting at church. We'll be back in an hour or so."

"Okay, Mom." Elizabeth closed the door and turned the key in the lock.

Elizabeth spun the chrome clover-shaped faucet handles. The spigot spat, the pipes groaned, and the water roared into the milky-white claw-footed tub. She wiggled her fingers under the waterfall to test the temperature, then pinned her hair up into a bun.

Cautiously she touched a toe to the water. Not too hot, not too cold—just right, like the littlest bear's porridge. She stepped into the tub and sat down, stretching her long legs as far as possible. The tub was too short and made bald islands of her knees. She put her head back, and the steam rose around her. The water licked at the bottom of her chin. Her body was prickly velvet. She closed her eyes and let her thoughts run.

Jeff wouldn't meet her at the Old Saw Mill. He wouldn't run away. Why should he? He didn't have weird parents who embarrassed him. He didn't know what it was like.

She looked across the still bath water. Though she hadn't moved, the water suddenly rippled as if someone had tapped the side of the tub with a tack-hammer. It settled again. She pushed a stray lock of hair away from her eyes and slid deeper into the water.

You don't know the first thing about surviving. You don't

know how to make any money. Your parents have always given you an allowance. Where will you go? What will you do? What's so terrible about your life that you want to run away?

You don't know, she answered the voice. *You don't understand.*

I know, the voice said. *I understand.*

Her internal argument made her feel tense again. She lifted up her right foot just as a drop of water fell from the tap. It splashed cold against her skin. She sighed and closed her eyes.

Suddenly rough hands grabbed her, hard fingers grasped her throat, pressing tight, pushing her under icy water.

Elizabeth gasped and opened her eyes. She glanced around. The bathroom was as it had been: stark and untroubled.

Where in the world did that come from? she wondered. She tried to re-construct the image in her mind, but it was a blur. Rough hands around her throat. No air. No breath.

How bizarre, she thought as she tried to calm down. She didn't usually have violent thoughts or imaginings, regardless of how tense she felt. *I'm just upset,* she concluded. She glanced down into the bath and instantly recoiled.

The water was filthy brown with bits of grass and sludge floating on top, as if a sewer had backed up through the drain. Her stomach turned, and she grabbed the sides of the tub to pull herself out. She pushed but couldn't get her footing on the slick porcelain. Her legs splayed out and she lost her grip, sending her body splashing downward, sliding toward the front of the tub. Her head dipped under the water and hit against the bottom. She thrashed out, her hands clawing at something, anything. She grabbed the edge, pulling herself up with all her strength, and catapulted herself over the side of the tub. The water spilled with her as she struck the cold tiled floor. She lay on her side, coughing and sputtering for a moment. She wanted to scream for her dad, but she couldn't find the breath.

What happened? How could—? Her mind was tangled with the impossibility of what had happened.

A dream. I must've fallen asleep in the bath and slipped under the water. Of course. I've been lying here for a long time. It's the only thing that makes sense.

On unsteady legs she stood up to dry herself. The pain in her side was already fading. Still, the violent image of rough hands strangling her flashed in and out of her mind like a flickering strobe. Rough hands, the strangling feeling, brown water.

She opened the door, wondering if her mom was still there.

The bedroom was dark.

Light spilled in from the bathroom, guiding her as she made her way to the dresser. She opened the top drawer and retrieved some panties. The T-shirt was next. In the closet, she found a robe, but it was unfamiliar to her. Probably one of her mother's re-sale shop finds. She put it on.

The house was strangely quiet. She sat down on the edge of the bed, trying to pinpoint why she felt so odd. A left-over feeling from what happened in the tub, perhaps.

She heard footsteps in the hall, and her skin went goose-pimply. Her parents were supposed to be at church.

There was a shadow of feet under the door.

"Mom?" she whispered, surprised at how her voice

caught in her throat.

The door slowly opened. Even by the dim light from the bathroom, she could make out the shape and shadowy details of the face.

It wasn't her mom. Or her dad.

Elizabeth put a hand to her mouth to stifle her cry even as the stranger glanced toward the bathroom, then suddenly snapped his head in her direction. His eyes grew wide.

They both screamed.

Here's a chapter from Time Twists 2, *Stranger in the Mist*

CHAPTER 3

Stranger in the Mist

A tall, gray old man stepped to the pinnacle of Glastonbury Tor, an unusual cone-like hill on which stood a tower named for a saint. In the wet English twilight, the wind whipped the old man's long gray hair and beard and his ragged brown monk's robe like a flag in a gale. The dark clouds above moved and gathered as if they thought him a curiosity worth investigating. Chalice Hill and Wearyall Hill waited in attendance nearby, their shoulders hunched like two old porters. The battered abbey beyond Chalice Hill listened in silence, unable to see from its skewered position.

The old man, a soloist before a strange orchestra, cast a sad eye to the green quilt littered with small houses and shops. They were an indifferent audience.

The old man prayed silently for a moment, then pulled an old curved horn from under his habit. He placed it to his lips and blew once, then twice, then a third time. The three muted blasts were caught by the wind and carried away.

The overture was finished, the program was just beginning.

"Look at that," Ben Hearn said to his wife, Kathryn. "It's crazy, I tell you. Crazy."

"What's crazy, Ben?" Kathryn suddenly asked, peering through the unusual fog.

"Didn't you see the sign for Malcolm Dubbs's village?"

Kathryn hadn't. But they were on one of the roads bordering the vast Dubbs estate, and she knew what sign her husband was talking about. It was the one that announced the construction of Malcolm Dubbs's Historical Village.

"I don't know what the town council was thinking when they agreed to it," Ben said. Malcolm was the most wealthy citizen of their little town of Fawlt Line. In fact, his family had been there for close to two centuries. Malcolm, a history buff, had designated a large portion of his property for the village.

Kathryn squinted at the fog ahead. "Don't you think you should slow down? It's getting thicker."

The truck engine whined as Ben heeded his wife. "You know what he's doing with the village, right? He's shipping in *buildings*. Brick by brick and stone by stone from all over the world. Have you ever heard of such a thing? A museum with a few trinkets and artifacts I could understand, but buildings?"

Kathryn smiled. "Malcolm always was obsessed with history. I remember when we were in school together—"

Ben wasn't listening. "Do you know what they've been working on for the past few weeks? Some kind of a ruin from England. A monastery or castle or cathedral, I don't know for sure."

"From England?" Kathryn asked, instantly lost in the romance of the idea. Then she grinned. "Did he have this fog shipped in too?"

Ben grunted, "I just don't understand Malcolm's fascination with something that's ruined. What's the point?"

Kathryn was about to answer—and would have—if a man on horseback hadn't suddenly appeared on the road in front of them. The fog cleared just in time for Ben to see him, mutter an oath as he hit the brakes, and jerk the steering wheel to the right. The horse reared wildly, and the rider flew backward to the ground. Kathryn cried out as the truck skidded into a ditch on the side of the road and came to a gravel-spraying stop. Ben and Kathryn looked at each other shakily.

"You all right?" Ben asked.

Kathryn nodded.

"Of all the stupid things to do—" Ben growled and angrily pushed his door open. The angle of the truck threatened to spring it back on him. He pushed harder and held it in place as he crawled out. "Stay here," he said before the door slammed shut again.

Kathryn reached over and turned on the emergency flashers.

The on-and-off yellow light barely penetrated the fog that swirled around Ben's feet. He made his way cautiously down the road. "Fool," Ben muttered to himself, then called out. "Hello? Are you all right?"

The fog parted as if to show Ben the man lying on the side of the road.

"Oh no," Ben said, rushing forward. He crouched down next to the figure. Whoever it was seemed to be wrapped in a dark blanket. He was perfectly still. Even in the darkness, Ben could tell he was a bear of a man. His face was hidden in the fog and shadows.

"Hey," Ben said, hoping the man would stir. Ben looked

him over for any sign of blood. Nothing was obvious around his head. But what could he expect to see in the darkness? "Kathryn!" he shouted back toward the car. "Bring me the flashlight from the glove compartment!"

He peered closely at the shadowed form of the man as he heard Kathryn open her door. *What's the guy doing in a blanket? Why's he riding a horse so late in the evening? Why would anyone dash across a road thick with fog?* The crunch of his wife's shoes on the gravel came closer. The shaft of light from the flashlight bounced around eerily in the ever-moving fog.

Kathryn joined him and beamed the light at the stranger. He had long dark salt-and-peppery hair, beard, and mustache and a rugged, outdoorsy kind of face. Anywhere from forty to sixty years old, Ben figured. He wore a peaceful expression. He could've been sleeping.

"He's not dead, is he?" Kathryn asked, reacting in her own way to the peculiar serenity on the man's face.

"I don't think so." Ben reached down, separating the blanket to check the man's vital signs. The feel of the cloth told him it wasn't a blanket at all. As he pushed the fabric aside, he realized that it was a cape made of a thick coarse material, clasped at the neck by a dragon brooch. "What in the world—?"

Kathryn gasped.

They expected to see a shirt or a sweater or a coat of some sort. Instead the man wore a long vest with the symbol of a dragon stitched on the front, a gold belt, brown leggings, and soft leather footwear that looked more like slippers than shoes. The whole outfit reminded Ben of a costume in a Robin Hood movie. At the stranger's side was a sword in a sheath.

"Is it Halloween?" Kathryn asked.

Ben shook his head. "I think I'd better get the truck out of that ditch so you can go for help."